I0603972

CYNTHIA HICKEY

To Snap A Killer

A Hollywood Murder, Book 5

Cynthia Hickey

Copyright © 2019 Cynthia Hickey
Published by: Winged Publications

This book is a work of fiction. Names, characters, places, and incidents are the product of the author's imagination and are used fictitiously. Any resemblance to actual events, locales, or persons, living or dead, is coincidental.

No part of this book may be copied or distributed without the author's consent.

All rights reserved.

ISBN-13: 978-1-0881-9472-0

DEDICATION

To All Those who love a good "Who done it"

.

Dear Reader,

I'd only planned four books in this series originally, but with Kelly's father's murderer on the loose, I had one final crime to solve. While this story is shorter, I felt it needed to be told. I hope you enjoy. If so, please leave a review on this and any of the other books you may have read. Reviews are an author's lifeblood.

Cynthia

Chapter One

I, Kelly Canyon, actor and novelist, returned to my roots. After the murder of Robert and Lana Doyles, and the attempt on Hollywood's newest hunk, Lance Cruz, the filming on my crime drama television series was on hiatus. Now was the perfect time to hunt down the man who killed my father.

My grandmother, Ruthie, stayed busy planning her wedding, my own Hollywood hunk, Brock "Handsome" Hanson was filming on location in Australia and wouldn't return for a few more days. Now was the perfect opportunity to get into trouble with my trusty sidekick and German Shepherd, Shutterbug.

So, here I was, hiding in the bushes behind the mansion that once belonged to the deceased Doyles, but now belonged to crime boss, Martin Rossi. I snapped photo after photo of him swimming in the pool, pacing the deck, and talking on his cell phone. I had no proof, but my gut told me he was the one responsible for my father's death more than ten years ago. All I needed was evidence.

Shutterbug's head whipped to the side. Her ears stood as straight as soldiers. Rossi had a visitor.

I hesitated. Should I stay or go? My intuition said, *stay*. Can I mention I wasn't surprised to see Cheryl Downs, the pretty little chef of the now-deceased Robert Doyles? An opportunist, she seemed to have moved from one sugar daddy to another, if the heated kiss she gave him was any indication. Gross. The man had to be thirty years older. I nabbed a couple of photos and crept from the bushes back to where my 1970 Aqua Camaro convertible waited in front of nosy Iris Beacon's house.

If you needed information on someone and couldn't find it, the aging movie star was the one to go to. She peered over her privacy fence. "Steamy, isn't it? Shameful." She grinned.

"It's disgusting." I clipped Shutterbug into the front passenger seat.

"That isn't the only little chickadee flitting around him." She wiggled her thinly-tweezed, penciled-on eyebrows.

"Do tell." I returned her grin and leaned against the car. "Although gossip is wrong, my friend."

"Not gossip if it's the truth." She lowered her voice. "That agent, Hilga, comes by regularly. That's not rumor, but this is. I heard from the grocery delivery boy that he heard Rossi wants to be in the movies."

"Really?" I frowned. "That doesn't make sense."

"I know. Some people will never have enough money."

It wasn't the acting. Rossi had to have his mind set on something bigger. What if he tried to purchase the studio from the elusive Eric James Johnson III? If Rossi put the hit out on my father and bought the studio, a target could very well be put on Ruthie and me.

"Gotta go, Iris. Thanks." Rushing to the driver's side, I jumped in and sped home. I burst through the front door. "Ruthie!"

"Outside."

I found her lounging by the pool. "Did you hear that Rossi wants to join the Hollywood scene?"

She pulled down her large sunglasses and peered over the top. "As in movies?"

"That's what Iris said she heard from someone who heard from someone."

"Then it's reliable. The grapevine is usually accurate." She replaced her glasses on the bridge of her nose. "Do you think he's wanting to buy property here? Expand past Vegas?"

I plopped into the chair next to her. "It crossed my mind."

This time she fully removed her glasses. "That wouldn't be good, Kelly. With you suspecting him of killing Kevin, having him so close to us all the time…well, he did kind of threaten you a few months ago at Lana's dinner party."

How could I forget? I'd dressed up, preparing myself to flirt with the man—which I was horrible at by the way—only to have the man see through my ruse and admit to having known my father. Sometimes I thought my dad had been the only honest officer left on the force. Then I'd met Lori Lawrence who had been his girlfriend at the time of his death and realized there had been at least two on the up and up. Lori and I were now close friends and worked together to find his killer. Along with Lori and me was my new-found half-brother, the son of one of Dad's even earlier girlfriends. Life was complicated.

"I guess we'll have to wait and see." I leaned back and closed my eyes. "How's the wedding planning coming?"

She smiled. "Amazing. We're right on target for next weekend's celebration." She faced me, her lips pressing together. "Don't ruin my wedding with any dead bodies, Kelly."

I'd laugh at her remark if it didn't ring true. Most of the time when Ruthie threw a party, someone ended up dead. "Where's Morgan?"

"Tux-fitting. He's starting to stress about Brock being gone so long."

"He'll be here in time." My honey had yet to let me down on anything. Hollywood's Golden Boy was as good inside as he was gorgeous. I smiled remembering his proposal. I'd said yes, but asked him to wait to make the announcement until the excitement of Ruthie's wedding was over. He'd sweetly agreed.

"What's so funny?"

"I'm not laughing."

Ruthie made a noise in her throat. "You look as

if you're up to something."

"Not me." I feigned surprise.

"Whatever."

A shadow fell over us. I opened my eyes to see Morgan staring down at his future bride. He'd been in love with my grandmother since he'd first seen her years ago as an exotic dancer. Then, she'd gotten her big break at acting, and here we all were.

Morgan leaned down and kissed Ruthie. "What are you two up to?"

She explained our conversation. Morgan frowned. "Looks like I'll be playing bodyguard again."

"Sweetheart, you'll have to keep me out of trouble for the rest of your days." Ruthie patted his cheek. "You'll love every minute of it."

"When you aren't scaring the daylights out of me, yes." He kissed her again. "I picked up my tux. It didn't need further alteration, so I need to put it away. I'll have Sarah fix us a tray of tea and I'll join you in a few."

"Sounds wonderful. Have her make sandwiches, too."

"Way ahead of you. I know how to do my job." Sarah Doyles, the former wife of the dead Robert Doyles, became our new chef after keeping me alive when I had to hide out as a homeless person. We'd shared the comfy area under a bridge for a few weeks, then I'd brought her home

Did I mention Ruthie and Sarah have a love/hate relationship?

Sarah set the tray on a patio table, then returned to the house. But not before sending Ruthie a glare.

"Oh, and you have company. Lisa is in the restroom. I'll send her out here."

"Thank you," I said. Good. Not only was Lisa my makeup artist but also a close friend and a computer genius. If something was on the internet, she could find it or hack into it. Nothing was safe from her. She really should be working for the FBI.

I headed into the house. I'd rather talk to her about Rossi without Morgan hearing, so when Lisa exited the bathroom, I asked, "Want to go get a coffee somewhere private?"

She tilted her head. "Not a coffeeshop or here, then."

"Nope. We'll pick up our coffee and take it to the studio." I grabbed my purse before hooking Shutterbug's leash to her collar. My fur baby was the best warning system a girl could have.

Over thirty minutes later, I parked in the lot, and we made a beeline for the trailer. Inside, we sat on the sofa with our legs curled under us and sipped our coffee. I explained the rumor I'd heard about Rossi and the pictures I'd taken. "I'd like you to see what you can find out."

"That shouldn't be hard. The man isn't exactly a private person." She took another sip of her hot mocha drink. "I can have Lance keep an ear open around the studio."

"That's right. He's filming a new sitcom. Perfect." Lance Cruz and Lisa hooked up during the Doyles mystery. Since he'd been shot by his biological mother, Lisa stuck close to his side. "Make sure he's discreet. I don't think he'd enjoy getting shot again."

She shuddered. "Don't remind me. I'll start digging around tonight. Now, about Cheryl—" She smiled.

"What have you heard?" I straightened.

"Everyone knows Doyles left her money. You must be the last person around here to know she is now the latest arm candy for Rossi. No more chef coats for her. She's dressing in Armani gowns. Not only that—" she wiggled her eyebrows, "I don't think it's Rossi who wants in the movies."

"Cheryl?" I thought she'd wanted to be a chef.

"Yep. Rossi has been kissing up to Hilga on Cheryl's behalf."

"Hmm." I sat back to digest the information. Relief trickled through me. If he was hanging around because of the young woman, then there probably wasn't a target on me or Ruthie. I'd have to be careful not to let him know I was digging into his life. "You are quite the fountain of information."

She shrugged. "It's a hobby of mine."

"The strange thing is that Rossi and Hilga were already chummy. Remember the conversation we overheard of him wanting Hilga to get her hands on Doyles' money so he could be repaid for the man's debt? Why not just threaten her to sign Cheryl? It's how he usually does business."

Shutterbug huffed low in her throat and stared at the trailer door.

Lisa climbed up on her knees to glance out the window. "Why not ask him?"

I got up and followed her gaze. Rossi and Hilga hovered in the empty space between two trailers across from us. I ducked and jerked Lisa down.

"Don't let them see you."

"How are we going to hear what they're saying?"

"I don't know, but they can't know we're here." The last thing I wanted was for someone to tell Brock I'd been shot dead in my makeup trailer.

After we were certain they'd left, mainly because Shutterbug settled down, we slipped out the trailer door and giggled our way to the car.

"I have so much fun around you," Lisa said. "Do you think the wedding will go off without a murder?"

I crossed my fingers and held my hand high. "I hope so."

Chapter Two

"Oh, Grandma." Tears shimmered in my eyes. "You look beautiful."

Gorgeous in a cream wedding dress that fit tight in the bodice and flared out at the hips, Ruthie looked as if she'd stepped out of a 1950s fashion magazine. A dainty hat with a veil perched on top of her red hair. She beamed. "I'll let the grandma comment slide today. You look very nice, too, sweetie."

I ran a hand down the simple strapless silk gown of royal blue. "We do clean up nice. Are you ready?" Not only was I standing up with her, but I would be the one giving her to Morgan. I couldn't say giving *away*, since we'd all still live together. They planned on a simple honeymoon at the beach, returning in a couple of days. I'd wanted to pay for a trip to Europe, but they insisted home was where they wanted to be.

"I'm ready." She picked up an extravagant bouquet of white roses with greenery and baby's breath that cascaded around her hands. The dress might be simple elegance, but the flowers were not.

I crooked my arm, holding the smaller spray of flowers in my right hand. "Let's get you respectable for the first time in your life."

"Don't bring up my past. I'm a new woman." She chuckled. "How I wish your father could have been here."

"Me, too." I blinked back tears and escorted my grandmother to the edge of the white carpet runner laid across our lawn.

Two hundred people stood as an organist played the first notes of the wedding march. It wasn't easy holding Ruthie to a sedate pace, but I managed. When I handed her over to Morgan, all three of us had tears in our eyes. I glanced over at Brock, the best man, and smiled as he tossed me a wink. Soon, we could announce our own engagement and make plans for a much simpler affair. No massive white party tents for us. A simple event on the beach would be all we needed.

I yanked my attention away from my wedding dreams and focused on the couple saying their vows. Morgan's voice shook as he repeated after the pastor. Ruthie's rang strong and true. She might have had cold feet a month ago, but they'd warmed. I couldn't be happier for her.

After the ceremony, I filled a plate from the buffet and sat next to Brock at the wedding table.

He'd only returned late last night from filming. "I missed you." I leaned over for a kiss.

"It wasn't easy waiting until now to see you." He kissed me harder, then straightened. "I know you'll be switching from maid of honor to photographer, but I plan on a dance or two."

"Sounds wonderful." I lifted my champagne glass in the direction of the bride and groom. "They are beaming." I wasn't the only photographer at the event, so would be able to enjoy the reception. But, Ruthie said no one captured candid shots the way I did and insisted. I didn't mind. I felt more at home behind a camera than in front of one.

Heads turned and conversations ceased as Rossi, with Cheryl on his arm, sat at a table on the outside edge of the tent. I leaned close to Ruthie. "Why are they here?"

"So you can snoop, dear." She patted my hand. "I didn't want them at the ceremony, but the reception is okay. Besides, I heard Cheryl landed a small role in a film. They're one of us now."

I rolled my eyes. Still, a smile teased at my lips, and excitement competed with the champagne. A chance to eavesdrop by taking pictures. What I did best.

The band director announced the wedding party dance and Brock took my hand, leading me onto the dance floor. We watched for the first minute of the song. Ruthie didn't want a full dance for just her and Morgan, only a minute to get things started before we joined them. We foxtrotted onto the floor. My grandmother wasn't one for tradition, it turned out. When we'd finished, the contests converged on the floor, and I went to retrieve my camera from under the wedding table.

I moved around the dance floor snapping photographs until I reached the table where Lori and my brother, Jason, sat. Partners on the police force, they promised to help keep order at the wedding. "I'm glad you two didn't wear your suits. Scoot close." I snapped their photo.

"I did." Jason fluttered a blue tie at me.

"I have a couple of dresses in my closet," Lori said. "But no heels." She held up a foot wearing a shiny black ballet flat. "What's Rossi doing here?"

I explained about Cheryl nabbing an acting gig. "Ruthie said it would give me a good opportunity to observe him."

"Clever." Lori smiled. "I'll watch from the sidelines and try to find some pretty young girl for Jason to dance with."

His eyes widened. "I don't dance. I'm happy sitting here with you."

"You sit with me every day. Find a woman."

"You are a woman."

"Old enough to be your mother." She laughed and scanned the dancing crowd. "Maybe your little sister has a friend."

I joined in the laughter. "The only friend I have is interested in Lance. I'll catch up with the two of you later. Have fun."

"Try not to stumble over any dead bodies," Lori called after me.

I winced. If everyone kept saying that, they were going to jinx me.

Someone called my name. I whirled to see

Cheryl grinning like a maniac. "Did you hear? I'm going to be in your television show."

"What?" I narrowed my eyes. "I thought you were going to be in a film."

"That's a film."

"Not the same, Cheryl. What part?"

Rossi's arm slid around his girlfriend's waist. "She's going to be a rookie who causes you a lot of problems. Won't that be fun?" His smile didn't quite reach his eyes.

"Like real life," I smirked. "You caused a few problems in the investigation into the Doyles case, if I remember correctly."

"That was not my fault. Everything that happened there had been put into place by Robert." She lifted her chin. "Now I have Martin." She squeezed his arm. "He's a true gentleman and a one-woman-at-a-time man."

Sure he was. "I'm happy for you. Did you end up signing with Hilga?"

"Yes, she is wonderful. Well, we need to mingle. I've a career to get started, and knowing the right people is the best thing I can do."

I met Rossi's sharp gaze. "I'm pretty sure knowing Rossi is all you'll need to move up. Ciao." I could feel his gaze on me as I marched away and fought back a shudder.

Tangling with such a man could very well be the most dangerous thing I've ever done. Still, Dad deserved justice, and I intended to see that he got it. I spotted Hilga, cell phone to her ear, but staring at the couple I'd just left. I snapped a couple photos of her unhappy face, then headed in her direction.

Maybe I could find out exactly how thrilled—or not—she was about signing Cheryl.

"Congratulations on your new acquisition," I said.

She frowned and got off the phone. "What are you blabbering bout?"

"Cheryl. You signed her, right? Got her a part on *The Hart of Crime*?"

"Oh, right." She shrugged. "She isn't bad."

"But not good?" I raised my eyebrows. "I hope she doesn't bring down the show's rankings."

"She will." Hilga dropped heavily into a chair and propped her head on one hand. "What do you want, Kelly?"

"Nothing." I sat across from her. "Are you all right?"

She sighed. "Do you believe in God?"

"Of course. Why?"

"I've been rethinking my life. Maybe I'll start going to church." She turned her head. Her gaze followed the mingling progression of Rossi and Cheryl. "I've done some dirty deeds in my time."

"God can forgive them."

"Maybe." She shrugged. "Anyway, you wouldn't be sitting with me if you didn't want something. Talk."

"Okay." I grinned. "How do you really feel about those two?" I motioned my head toward Rossi and Cheryl.

"I fancied myself in love with him once. The girl is worthless. She'll flit from one moneybags to another."

"You were forced to sign her, weren't you?"

Her features settled into a mask. She made the motion of locking her lips and throwing away the key.

I was no dummy. I could read between the lines. Whatever Rossi held over Hilga's head had caused her to sign Cheryl, then he must have used the same force on Louie to get the woman assigned to the show. "What does he have on you?"

She crossed her arms. "Don't ask questions you know I can't answer." She leaned forward, spearing me with a gaze. "Watch your back. Don't trust Chief Warren, and spend some time at You Store 'Em, storage room 111." She sprang up, slapped her hands flat on the table, and raised her voice. "Stop asking questions. It won't go well for you."

What the heck? I watched her storm away, then noticed Rossi glaring in our direction. Ah, her sudden change to aggression had been an act. Very well. I could act, too. I pretended to be dejected and fumbled with my camera. I gave Rossi a sheepish grin, looked chastised, and shuffled back to the wedding party table.

Brock returned from dancing with Lori and took his seat next to me. "What's wrong?"

"Nothing," I whispered. "It's just an act."

"O-kay." He drew out the word, clearly confused. "You can tell me all about it later. Learn anything new?"

I smiled. "I suddenly need to rent a storage unit."

"We're definitely talking later."

A scream rang out, then a shout of laughter and a splash. The partiers had moved to the pool. Ruthie had advised bringing swimsuits, even had changing tents set up with suits in different sizes for those who forgot. She'd thought of everything. If Ruthie hadn't turned to acting after dancing, she could have been a hit at party planning.

Flushed, she fell into the seat next to me. "I couldn't be happier. It's a great party, and isn't Morgan the handsomest thing you've ever seen?"

"The second handsomest." I caressed Brock's cheek. "And, yes, it's a super reception."

"I'm not getting in the pool, but I am going to change into that new bathing suit I bought." She gulped down water in a crystal goblet, then pushed to her feet. "You should change, too. You'll be more comfortable."

"Good idea." I grabbed Brock's hand. "Let's go get casual."

Ruthie changed into a cream-colored one piece that laced up the back. She'd bought me a matching royal blue one, saying it was important for our suits to match our gowns. Okay. Filmy sarongs and sandals completed the look. Then, we headed for the pool. You could barely see the water for the bodies.

"Good thing you didn't want to go in," Brock said. "Shouldn't there be a limit to how many people can go in at once?"

"I think so." I glanced to where Lori frowned at the crowd.

Someone screamed.

The crowd parted.

Floating face down, blood pooling around her, was Hilga. A knife protruded from her back. I had a feeling she wasn't faking her death as Robert

Doyles had tried to do.

As one, the crowd bolted from the pool.

At the edge, a stony-faced Rossi and a shocked Cheryl stared at the body.

Chapter Three

"No!" Cheryl buried her face in Rossi's shirt. "My career."

My thoughts toward her selfishness weren't charitable. I glared in their direction, meeting Rossi's stare.

Jason jumped into the water and checked for a pulse. "She's dead." He glanced at Lori.

Lori shook her head.

Ruthie collapsed into a pool chair. "Why does this always happen? I'm not having any more parties."

Poor Hilga. Tears burned my eyes. She had to have expected something or why ask me about God? I prayed she'd made her peace as I moved to Lori's side. "I spoke to her before changing into my suit, and she'd been on the phone with someone. If you find out who, you might get a clue about who killed her." I lowered my voice. "I've more to say when we're alone."

She nodded and pointed to a rectangle at the bottom of the pool. "That phone?"

"Oh."

"We might be able to retrieve something, but I'm not hopeful." She cupped her hands around her mouth. "No one leaves until we've questioned you." She motioned for Jason to secure the front entrance. "Clear the house, would you, Brock?" She pulled a phone from her pocket and called for reinforcements.

I put an arm around Ruthie's shoulders. "It's just bad luck. We aren't jinxed or anything." Funny. Poor Hilga. I settled back in the chair next to my grandmother, preparing myself for the long wait to be questioned—something that was becoming an unwelcome habit.

Morgan gave Ruthie a quick kiss. "I'm going to help with crowd control. Will you be all right?"

"Kelly is here. Where's Sassy?"

"Right here." Sarah carried the Yorkie to Ruthie. Behind her trotted Shutterbug, and Brock's mastiff, Brutus. "These three were going crazy inside the house. Too bad they can't talk. They may have seen the crime happen."

Lori's head whipped in her direction. "Say that again?"

She repeated what she'd said. "Shutterbug went from zero to sixty in frenzied barking."

"Where's her leash? Kelly, walk your dog in the crowd. See how she reacts."

My dog was smart, but not smart enough to tell us who killed Hilga. But, it was worth a try. I followed orders, made sure Sassy snuggled up with Ruthie, and kept my gaze sharp on my dog.

Shock, tears, and murmurs greeted us as we mingled. Under the pretense of making sure everyone was all right, I went from cluster to cluster while Shutterbug sniffed around feet and consoled when she could. Most of the guests were happy to pat or hug her. Her tail wagged the entire time. Not one person raised her hackles.

Maybe it wasn't about my dog. Maybe Lori used it as a ruse for me to overhear conversations. Either way, the effort failed. I learned nothing. Except…I turned, spotting Rossi and Cheryl on the patio. His arm rested around her shoulders as she wailed about no longer having an agent. I led Shutterbug to them.

She poked her nose under Cheryl's arm, causing the woman to shriek in fear. "Get it away. Dogs scare me."

"She won't hurt you." I didn't move. "She's making sure you're all right."

"Do I look all right?" Her voice rose. "My career is ruined before it began."

"You signed a contract, dear." Rossi rubbed her back. "You still have the show, and we'll find you another agent."

"Oh." The tears stopped as if someone had shut off a switch.

Shutterbug wasn't interested in Rossi one way or the other. In fact, she acted as if the man wasn't there. What a good judge of character. I smiled. "My dog doesn't like you, Mr. Rossi."

"The feeling is mutual. Animals are worthless unless you're going to eat one." He plucked a dog hair off his dark pant leg. "Messy things. Why not put it to good use and find out who killed Hilga?"

"That's exactly what I'm doing." I laughed, meeting his shrewd look. "Does that make you nervous?"

His returning laugh lacked humor. "You shouldn't taunt me, Miss Canyon. While you are a pretty thing, that pert little nose goes where it shouldn't. What would this city do without one of its favorite actors?"

My blood chilled. I wasn't sure if he was threatening me or Brock. "I don't plan on getting involved in Hilga's death. I have much bigger fish to catch." Doing my best to portray a confidence I didn't feel, I marched away, my grip firm on my dog's leash.

If Rossi killed Hilga, Cheryl would have to be in on it, but I felt that her shock and grief were real. That meant if he was the responsible person, he'd have someone else do the dirty deed. But who?

I stood on the fringes of the crowd and searched for someone who looked guilty or overly interested in the actions of law enforcement at the party. Nobody drew my attention, so I turned to the hired caterers. Most of Staletti's workers were familiar, but he'd obviously brought in extras to help cover the wedding. I focused my attention on them.

Five young men in black pants and starched white shirts lingered around the buffet table. Despite their attempts to clean up the leftover food and dirty dishes, every one of them cast furtive glances to where the arriving police gathered around the body. Some might be nervous because of prior felonies or misdemeanors, but one of them might be the killer.

I know I'd said I wouldn't investigate Hilga's death, but if Rossi killed her—and I strongly suspected he did—then her death could be related to Dad's. So I convinced myself that by digging into this murder, I was actually working on solving his.

"Is there anything you need?" I pasted on a smile. "I doubt you thought this would happen when you signed on for the job."

"That's the truth." A brown-haired young man with dark eyes and olive skin scowled, "We'll be here all night."

"Yes, death is an inconvenience." I frowned. Sometimes, people's self-centeredness really grated on me. "Did any of you see anything suspicious?"

"You a cop?" He took a step back.

"No, I live here. I'm trying to be a good hostess."

He turned to the others. "See anything?"

They all shook their heads, except for one. He spun around and headed for the fence.

"Hold up. Don't make me sic the dog on you." I released the leash.

Shutterbug fixed her eyes on the man who now sprinted for an escape.

"Hold him, girl." I waved my hand.

Shutterbug took off, catching up with the young man as he leaped for the top of the fence. She clamped her teeth on the leg of his pants and pulled him to the ground where she stood guard, teeth bared.

By now, Lori and Jason had joined us and had the man in cuffs. "I know you," Lori said, hauling him to his feet. "Daniel Mason. He has a rap sheet a mile long, but he's never resorted to violence before."

"I didn't kill anyone," he said. "But, there is a warrant out for my arrest."

If he didn't kill anyone— "Where's the young man I was talking to?"

Daniel glanced around me. "Richie? He's headed for the house."

Sure enough, with an empty tray in his hand and a sneaky glance over his shoulder, the other man, Richie, headed to the kitchen. He caught us watching and bolted. Shutterbug now had a new target and was on him before he could open the door.

Rossi and Cheryl watched with amusement as the man plastered himself to the wall. "Idiot," Rossi said. "They've locked the doors to keep us all in one place."

"Call off the dog." Richie's voice rose to a shriek.

"Down, girl." I clipped the leash on her collar as Jason cuffed the man and shoved him into a chair.

"Mr. Rossi, Miss Downs, some privacy, please." Jason motioned his head for them to leave.

With a long-suffering sigh, Cheryl rolled her eyes and stormed away. Rossi shoved his hands into his pockets and strolled after her, seemingly without a care in the world. In fact, he acted as if the murder was nothing more than party entertainment.

"Did you kill Hilga Smithwick?"

"Who?" Richie wrinkled his brow and glanced from her to me back to her.

"The body in the pool." Lori's face reddened.

"I'm not sure." He closed his eyes. "If I did, it was an accident."

Lori blinked rapidly. "You don't know if you stabbed her in the back?" She held up a clear bag containing a steak knife covered with blood. "Do you recognize this?"

"It looks like a knife we use." Sweat soaked through his shirt.

"Mr. Wilson, you're under arrest for the murder of Hilga Smithwick." Lori read him his rights. "Is your memory refreshed?"

"Fine." He paled. "I got a call from somebody who said if I didn't want anything to happen to my mother that I would have to do a job. Usually, a job is to steal something or sell a drug, so I said yes. But this time, he told me to kill that woman. I could hear my mother in the background crying. I didn't have a choice."

Color me confused. Rossi had been here the whole time. How could he call this man with a crying woman in the background?

"Where's your phone?" Lori asked.

"At the bottom of the pool. The man on the other end said to get rid of it."

"Then, where is Hilga's phone?" I asked. "Did she bring a purse?"

"Jason, lock this man up. We need to look for something we've missed." She glanced to where Hilga lay on the pool deck. "She's wearing yellow.

A purse that matches maybe?"

"Or a white one or a multi-colored one. It could be any color," I said. "It doesn't matter anymore. This isn't 1950."

Lori groaned. "Her phone is here somewhere."

I led Shutterbug to the body. She sniffed around, then glanced at me. "I know, girl. We're kind of doing this backward." I unhooked her leash. "Find."

She whined and glanced back at Hilga. Just when I thought my idea wouldn't work, Shutterbug headed for a flower bed at the opposite end of the lawn. She nosed around, then moved to a bush, then a tree. This wasn't going to work. I recognized bathroom behavior when I saw it.

Leaving my dog to her business, I strolled the perimeter of the yard, picking up dropped napkins as I went. I circled around to the back of the tent, picked up a dropped cigarette butt, a marijuana joint, and a plastic red cup that smelled strongly of alcohol. I started to think Richie had needed to work up quite a bit of courage in order to commit murder. Just as I turned to head back to the others without Hilga's purse, a flash of gold sparkles under an oleander bush caught my eye.

I knelt down and peered under the thick branches. Lying in the wood chips was a gold clutch with its contents spilled out. No phone, but the open wallet showed Hilga's driver's license. Someone had dumped the purse and taken the phone. Leaving everything where it lay, I rushed to Ruthie's side.

"Call Hilga's phone. Hurry. Before the police start releasing people."

Chapter Four

"Some people have already been released," Morgan shouted as he raced for the gate, me on his heels.

Ruthie called out that the phone was ringing. I stopped and strained my ears to hear the electronic sound of a phone. Hilga's ringtone was nothing fancy. There. I got to my knees near the pool pump. Behind it rang the phone. Drat.

Amid curses and complaints, Morgan blocked the gate. "Just relax, people."

Lori stood next to him. "Don't touch that phone, Kelly." She frowned in my direction, then directed Jason to bag the item and take it to the station.

As if I hadn't learned by then not to touch potential evidence. I pursed my lips and crossed my arms, acting a bit like a petulant child. It had been a long day.

"I expect everyone here to come to the station in the morning to be fingerprinted," Lori told the crowd. "I have a list of your names. Do not make me hunt you down. You may go home."

Once the last guest left, the rest of us collapsed on the patio furniture, too wound up to go to bed. Sarah brought out a pot of coffee.

"This brings back unpleasant memories," I said. While Robert floating face down in the pool had been a ruse to try and get insurance money, it had shown how much Sarah love/hated him. "Sit with us."

"No, but thank you, Kelly. I am tired. See you in the morning." She shuffled to her cottage, once our guesthouse, and closed the door against our conversation.

"I'm not throwing any more parties." Ruthie poured coffee.

"Good," Lori said. "You attract bad things when you do." Her eyes widened as Ruthie's filled with tears. "I'm sorry. That was a bad joke. This wasn't a very good ending to your wedding day."

"No, it wasn't." Morgan stood and took Ruthie's hand. "We have a honeymoon to get to. The rest of you can serve your own coffee." He cupped my grandmother's face. "Go get your suitcase, love."

She nodded and sniffed, then left. Morgan glared at his sister. "Not cool."

"I didn't mean it like it sounded." Lori ran a hand roughly through her hair. "I'm exhausted. I have my suspicions about who's behind the murder, but have no proof."

"Rossi killed Hilga and my father." I blew into my drink. "I know it deep inside me. We'll prove it, too."

"He is not a man to mess with." Morgan glanced from Lori to me. "Pure evil."

I returned his stare, refusing to back down. I knew what Rossi was and would do everything in my power to make sure justice was served.

"It's like talking to two brick walls." He shook his head. "Try to stay alive until I return from my honeymoon, please. Lori, you're going to get fired if you keep on this path."

She shrugged. "Then I'll be a private investigator. No big deal, big brother. I'm doing this with Kelly."

"Don't forget Hilga said not to trust the chief. I plan on going to the storage unit after I sleep a while. Lori is in a prime position right now to watch Chief Warren," I said. "Risky, but—"

Morgan sighed. "Do what you want." He met Ruthie at the French doors. "See y'all in a few days."

I watched as he escorted my grandmother from our property and smiled. My pleasure quickly faded. A day Ruthie had looked so forward to was now tainted by violence, death, and deceit. She deserved a wedding as beautiful as she was. "Somehow, we need to give Ruthie back what she lost. The perfect ending to her wedding day."

"How?" Brock crossed his long legs at the ankles and yawned. "Not to be harsh, but what's done is done."

"Finding Dad's killer is a start. I'll think of

something." Maybe a tribute when Brock and I got married. It wasn't much more than a thought at this point, but I'd think of something. "Who's going with me to the storage unit?"

"Me." Brock and Lori spoke in unison.

"You might need a warrant," Lori said, "in which case, you'll need me. I'll make sure I have one in hand when I arrive no earlier than one. I'm beat." She pushed to her feet and shuffled away.

I fell asleep in Brock's arms on the oversized lounge chair, three dogs crowded around us. The day might not have been everything we'd hoped for, but the day after the wedding started out wonderful.

When the sun woke us four hours later, Brock cooked me a killer omelet. We sat at a table by the pool and waited for the rental company to arrive to take down the tent, tables and chairs. Soon, there'd be no sign a wedding or a murder had taken place. Sad, really. Hilga had been as abrasive as coarse sand, but she hadn't deserved a knife in the back. My father hadn't deserved to be shot dead in the street either.

"What's whirling through your head?" Brock asked, pouring me a glass of orange juice.

"Hilga and Dad."

"All the pieces will fall into place. You're getting close. Too close. It scares me."

"I have to do this."

"I know." He gave me a sad smile. "I'll be right by your side the entire time."

I gave him a lingering kiss. "I know, and I love you for it."

Susan Gilroy, reporter for the *Hollywood*

Tribune, arrived on the heels of the rental company. "Another death at one of your parties? I'm starting to think you set these up, so you can write another book."

I'd been in life-or-death situations with Susan before, had competed for the same job before, but she grated on my nerves every time she came around. "I'm not telling you anything. Catch it on the news."

Without waiting for an invitation, she sat next to me. "Why are you like this? We aren't in competition anymore. For crying out loud, we were chased by a maniac."

"You're right. You also know I can't tell you anything during an ongoing investigation."

"Since when do you follow the rules?" She glanced at Brock. "Will you talk?"

He shrugged one shoulder. "I wouldn't want to risk the wrath of Kelly Canyon or Lori Lawrence. Sorry."

"I won an award for my write-up on Mildred Carson's murder of the Doyles. I'll figure this one out on my own." She marched out the gate.

That woman was going to get in my way, I just knew it.

Lori arrived right on time, warrant in hand. "Let's go before Chief Warren realizes I'm not at my desk writing up the report from last night."

"It'll probably take a while to go through the unit," I said, following her to a dark-colored sedan.

Brock graciously offered me the front passenger seat and climbed in the back with Shutterbug. With Morgan gone, he refused to let me out of his sight, big, beautiful, handsome man that he was.

It turned out we didn't need the warrant. The receptionist couldn't be pulled away from her soap opera enough to care. She told us that the unit had been rented under the name Sam Adams—clever, Dad—and of course, she had a spare key. She handed it over and returned her attention to the tiny television on her desk.

Lori scowled and led the way to unit number 111. She unlocked the padlock and stepped back for Brock to roll up the door. Inside were boxes and boxes. The kind copy paper came in. I stopped counting at twenty boxes.

"This is going to take a while." Lori grinned. "These must be every file he has on his last investigation. How did Hilga know?"

I shrugged as hope grew. "We should take these to the house and go through them there."

"I'll rent a truck from Ms. Congeniality." Brock jogged back to the reception office, returning with a U-Haul.

It took a couple of hours to load up all the boxes. Lori and I followed Brock back to the house.

"We're finally getting somewhere." I leaned my head against the back of the seat. We'd gone through a ton of boxes several months ago that had been stored in the shed of Ruthie's old house, and while it got us closer to the fact Dad's death wasn't a random act of violence, it didn't give us a name. I prayed these boxes would tell us not only who the dirty cops were but also who they worked for. I couldn't wait to dig in.

I groaned at the sight of Susan waiting in the

driveway. "I'm surprised you didn't stick around and try to follow us," I said the moment I climbed out of the car.

"No need to. It's obvious what's going on." She grinned and crossed her arms. "I knew if I waited around long enough, something would be revealed."

"And?" I raised my eyebrows.

"Brock Hanson is moving in with you. Looks like a couple of halos are getting tarnished."

"Sure. Go with that." I smiled and moved past her to stop Brock from opening the back of the U-Haul. It would be safer for all concerned to let her believe he'd packed up and brought his things. The last thing we needed was for Rossi or any of his goons to discover we had these files. Last time, we'd had a gang member pay us an unwelcome visit.

"Goodbye, Miss Gilroy." Lori's tone left no room for argument. "You cannot be at a crime scene."

"Fine." Susan strode to her car. "I *will* find out what's going on here. In the meantime, I'll print what I see and let people draw their own conclusions." She yanked her car door open and climbed inside, leaving tire marks on my driveway as she squealed away.

"I'm going to end up arresting her for obstruction of justice," Lori said.

I laughed. "Like you threaten me?"

"If anyone puts you behind bars again, it'll be the chief or one of the other officers." Her expression grew serious. "You have to keep your investigation low-key on this one. I know you won't stay out of things and I value your insight, but just keep it down."

I unlocked the front door and Brutus barged out, throwing himself against Brock. "It looks as if your best friend is missing you."

Brock rubbed the dog's ears. "No, this is something else. Where's Sassy?"

My heart stopped and I sprinted into the house calling for the Yorkie. Silence greeted me. Not a good thing where the little dog was concerned. Could she have run off because she missed Ruthie? But how would she have gotten out?

I rushed to the backyard. "Sassy."

Oh, Ruthie would be heartbroken. Where could the little pain-in-the-rear be?

"Find anything?" Brock joined me.

Brutus lumbered to a spot near the gate. We'd put wire through the bars when Sassy was a puppy to keep her from squeezing through, but now part of that wire had been cut. Sassy hadn't gotten away, she'd been taken.

"Look." I snatched a sheet of paper from under a rock and read aloud, "I love animals and don't want to harm the pup. I need some kind of assurance that you'll mind your own business. Give it to me when I call tonight, and I'll tell you where to pick up the dog."

I locked gazes with Brock and Lori. "What kind of assurance? How is a person supposed to give something like that? Is it the same as giving your word?"

Lori paced the walkway, muttering to herself. After a few minutes, she stopped as if the proverbial lightbulb had gone on over her head. "I've got it. We go through one of those boxes, make sure there isn't anything we need to know inside it, and offer it to him as returned evidence."

"Surely, Rossi would think we'd have more boxes," Brock said.

"It's all I've got."

"We're all saying the note is from Rossi," I pointed out. "The man wants money more than anything. Let's offer him some."

Lori shook her head. "He has more than enough. Do you have the negatives of the photos of the poker game in Las Vegas where Hilga helped him cheat?"

"Of course."

She grinned. "We'll give him those. He doesn't need to know there are copies at the precinct. My hope is these photos are important enough to him that he'll believe they're the best we have of his crimes."

Chapter Five

I slid the photos from Las Vegas into a large envelope, then into my camera bag. While we waited for a phone call that might or might not come, we tried to devise an organized way to go through the multitude of boxes.

"I guess we do it the same as last time," I said. "Grab a box and start digging."

"It's a bit different." Lori set a box on the dining room table. "Last time we did this, the boxes were full of family memorabilia. This time, it's police files." She cast a stern glance on us. "Complete confidentiality, you two. And be careful. I'm sure the archives at the station hold these same files, but if not, I'll need these as evidence when we convict Rossi."

'Duly noted." My cell phone rang. A glance at

the screen almost stopped my heart. "It's Ruthie. She's going to want to talk to Sassy."

"You're an actor. Fool her."

"I can't act like a dog."

Lori smirked. "Lie."

Brock carried in two boxes and set one in front of me. "Tell her the dog is out doing its business, then pretend you're losing connection. This is a right time for a falsehood. If we get Sassy back before Ruthie returns tomorrow night, she's none the wiser."

"Hey, how's the honeymoon?" I closed my eyes as if by doing so, I could cover up my lying.

"Wonderful. The weather is perfect, the water's gorgeous, and I have the handsomest man in the country. How are things there?"

"Great. We picked up the stuff from the storage unit and we're just about ready to dig in."

"How's my baby? She around?"

I took a deep breath and spewed, "she's outside doing her business. Can you hear me? You're breaking up. Hello?" I hit the red button.

Brock and Lori both stared at me as if my face had turned green. "Girl, it's a good thing you're a better actor than a liar. That was horrible." Lori laughed and removed the lid from her box.

Brock joined in the laughter. "I'm glad my girl can't lie. It's easy to trust her that way." He planted a kiss on the top of my head. "I always know what she's thinking."

"Really?" I raised my eyebrows. "Know what I'm thinking now?"

"Yep. That I'd better bring in some more boxes

and stay out of harm's way." He flashed a grin, drawing one of my own in return. Oh, I loved that man.

With cups of coffee in hand, we flipped through files. This would take days upon days upon weeks to get through them all. Good thing I was on a break from filming. I had a new full-time job. This felt too much like a desk job, and I hated desk jobs.

I paused in turning pages when I spotted Detective Sawyer's name. "Dad knew Sawyer was dirty."

Lori's head jerked up. "I wish he'd told me. Maybe I could have requested a different partner."

"Dad kept a lot of things from not only you, but his family." We hadn't known about his relationship with Lori or that he was investigating a string of bad cops. Now he was dead and all we had to go on were these files and gut instinct. "At least Jason is one of the good guys."

"Speaking of Jason, I've got to go. I forgot about that report. Warren will have my head. Call me if you hear from the dog-napper." She dashed out the door.

"This is going to take even longer with only the two of us." Brock took her place at the table. "We can't do it hour after hour, Kelly. We'll need breaks."

"I know." Already a headache threatened. Maybe we'd find something that warranted some street work. A girl could hope anyway.

For dinner, Brock ordered Chinese, but still no phone call came from the person who had Sassy. Worry rose in me like bamboo. When the call did come, I spilled my tiny glass of ginseng tea. The liquid spread toward the files.

"I'll get this. Answer the phone." Brock dabbed at the mess with napkins.

"Hello?" I put the phone on speaker.

An electronic voice answered. "Got something to convince me you'll not be nosy?"

"Yes."

"Good. Bring it to the Walk of Fame. Marilyn will be walking the dog." Click.

"Let's go." Brock grabbed his keys from the table by the door. "I'm driving. Here." He thrust something in my hand.

Sunglasses? I gave him a questioning look.

"Built-in camera." He grinned. "Just press the fake diamond on the temple to take a picture."

"Awesome." I slipped them onto my face and rather than take my entire camera bag, just grabbed the envelope. "I feel like a secret agent."

"I found this cool store downtown. I'll take you there sometime. All kinds of spy toys." He locked the house behind us, and once I belted Shutterbug and Brutus into the back seat of Brock's truck, we headed for Hollywood Boulevard and a date with Marilyn Monroe.

It took a while, but Brock finally found a place to park. He pulled a pair of sunglasses for himself from the glove compartment and pulled a baseball cap low over his eyes.

"Do you really think that's a disguise?" I shoved open my door. "Not only will we have to find the right Marilyn Monroe, we'll be fending off fans."

"It's the best I've got." He hooked a leash on

Brutus while I did the same with Shutterbug. "You didn't even try to disguise yourself."

"I don't see the point. Let's fight the masses and rescue a furry princess." I twisted Shutterbug's leash around my wrist. Uh-oh. I sent a quick text to Lori telling her what we heard and where we were.

Her response wasn't nice. *Try following directions for once.*

Brock put a hand on my lower back and led me into the throng of tourists and fans lining the street, taking pictures by the stars in the walk and by look-alikes who asked for donations. I'd had to meet up with crooks on this walk more times than I cared to admit. But when you could make a few easy dollars dressing up and hiding behind a mask, playing Spiderman or some other character could be the perfect hiding place right in the middle of hundreds of people.

Screams erupted as soon as someone spotted Brock. I smiled and tried to step to the side, only to have his grip on my waist tighten. "You aren't going anywhere, sweetheart." He grinned and greeted his fans. "I need the moral support."

Turns out that with the success of *The Hart of Crime*, my autograph was also sought. While I signed, I kept my eyes peeled for a Marilyn walking a Yorkie. There. By the theater. I nudged Brock. We signed faster, then excused ourselves, saying we'd be back in a few minutes.

We darted toward the woman who grabbed the Yorkie and shrank back at the sight of our two dogs. "Stay away."

"You have our dog."

Her heavily made-up eyes widened. "I do not. This is Precious. She's mine."

"I'm sorry." After looking closer at the dog, it became apparent it wasn't Sassy. Ruthie's dog wore a white collar covered with rhinestones. "Is there another Marilyn here with a Yorkie?"

"There's two." She marched away on ridiculous white stilettos.

"Can you tell us where?" I called after her.

Her only answer was rude gesture involving the middle finger. Real classy, Marilyn.

"We start walking." Brock took my hand.

Any progress was slow going as we found ourselves stopping regularly to sign autographs or take pictures. We should have come in costume.

"I see one." Brock pushed forward, dragging me with him. "Sometimes, I wish we'd trained our dogs to be a little more aggressive without a command to act. This crowd is ridiculous."

"You don't mean that." Although Shutterbug could bare her teeth instead of wagging her tail, couldn't she?

"You're right. I don't."

We broke free and approached the costumed woman. From the reaction of our dogs, I knew she held Sassy before we stopped in front of her.

"This envelope for the dog." I held out my hand.

"The man said you'd pay me a hundred dollars, too." She kept a firm grip on Sassy.

Seriously? I reached for my bag, then realized I'd not brought it.

"I'll get it." Brock paid the woman and snatched Sassy before she could demand something else.

I tilted my head. "You'll get the envelope in a minute. Who hired you?"

She shrugged. "I don't know. Some man in a hoodie came up to me and offered me a hundred dollars to watch a dog until Kelly Canyon came to retrieve it. Then you'd give me something and another one hundred dollars." She batted her eyelashes. "I didn't expect Brock Handsome to be with you. I'm one lucky gal."

I strongly suspected this particular Marilyn wasn't really a woman, but wisely held my tongue and snapped a few photos with my new toy. Why did nefarious people always wear hoodies? "Anything more you can tell me about the man who hired you?"

"Hispanic, I think. Could be white. Can you go now? You're taking the attention away from me, and a gal needs to make a living."

I handed Marilyn the envelope. She stuffed it under her dress.

With Sassy safely held under his arm, Brock led us back toward the car, stopping to sign the promised autographs, then insisted we had to go.

I ran my hands over Sassy checking for any injuries as Lori's squad car pulled up. The dog seemed fine and I helped Brock secure the other two in the truck.

"Well?" Lori asked after rolling down her window.

"Hired by someone else hired to hire them." I leaned against the truck. "Same old story. She knew nothing."

"Okay, but we'll likely hear back from the caller.

Next time, let me know before you take off. I can't make any arrests or further investigation if I'm not there. I'll meet you back at the house." She squealed tires, clearly showing her displeasure.

True to her word, Lori waited for us on the porch. I unlocked the door and went to fetch my laptop to upload the photos I'd taken. "Someone want to make coffee?"

"I will," Lori answered. "We should spend at least a couple hours going through the files."

A long day followed by a long night.

Sassy jumped on my leg, hopping like she was on a pogo stick. "Sorry, girl. Momma isn't home until tomorrow." I reached down to pet her. "Are you hungry?" I bent down to pick her up. A blank spot in her collar drew my attention.

A few of the rhinestones were missing. Ruthie was going to kill me. There would be no hiding the dog-napping now.

Chapter Six

"Well, this is a fine mess." Ruthie surveyed the boxes and papers spread across the dining table that could comfortably seat twelve. "Find out anything? Oh, there's my baby." She dropped her purse and knelt down to pick up her happy, squirming Yorkie. "You haven't had too much fun without me, have you?"

I held my breath and waited for the eruption. "Not…really."

Her gaze locked on me. "What happened to the diamonds in Sassy's collar?"

"Diamonds? They aren't rhinestones?"

"Of course they aren't rhinestones. I'm not an animal. My baby deserves the finest of everything."

"Maybe you should sit down," Lori said. "I think we all should." She muttered something about fools who had more money than they knew what to do with.

"I'll stand, thank you." Ruthie's features hardened, not softening even when Morgan joined us. "They're keeping something from us."

"Okay. Someone took Sassy from the backyard by cutting the fence. We had to go to Hollywood Boulevard last night and exchange information we knew about Rossi for her. My guess is Marilyn Monroe stole the diamonds."

"Way to vomit everything out." Lori crossed her arms. "We'll head back to the Walk of Shame and try to get back your diamonds, although I'm sure they're long gone."

"My baby was kidnapped?"

"Dog-napped," I said. "Kidnapped is—"

"Stop talking, Kelly." She glared. "I am so mad at you for not letting me know. We could have come home and helped you find her."

"Honey, let's sit down." Morgan helped her into a chair. "Everything is fine. Sassy is happy and unharmed. We were on our honeymoon. Lori is a police officer and capable of handling things." His narrowed eyes said he had his doubts. "Relax and let me pour you a glass of wine."

"Thank you." She glanced at the pile of boxes again. "Let's find the man who killed my son and took my Sassy. I want to see him hanged."

"We don't do that anymore," Lori said, pressing to her feet. "The photos of Marilyn, please."

I handed her copies. "Want company?"

"No, you're better used here. I'll be back as soon as I question this—" she stared harder at the pictures. "man." She shook her head. "Just one day I'd like things to be easy and make sense. With all these boxes to go through, I'll be living here until this case is over."

"I'll make up a guestroom." Good. Lori was a workhorse. She'd pore through the boxes and know better what information was helpful than I would.

The rest of us read page after page until Lori came back without the diamonds. "No sign of Mr. Monroe either. But we do have a body in a nearby park." She tossed the crime-scene photos on the table. "I'm thinking this is our Marilyn without the makeup. A loose end tied up."

"What about the man in the hoodie?"

She tossed another photo on the table of a young Hispanic man next to a dumpster. "Another loose end."

My heart dropped to my knees. "Warnings in regard to the envelope?"

"Maybe." She perched on a corner of the table. "If Rossi is behind this, he's playing games with us. People are expendable to men like him. He'll use them and toss them."

"He has no intention of letting us pin anything on him." Despite the increasing danger to my life, I would bring this man to justice. "What's our next step?"

Brock groaned. "Why did I know you were going to ask that?"

"Because you know me so well."

The doorbell rang. With her hand on her gun, Lori answered the door, letting Lisa in.

"I found something." She set her laptop on the

table and lit up the monitor. "Somebody filmed a meeting between Rossi and Hilga. They're afraid and posted this online in a secret chat room."

"What kind of chat room?" Lori peered closer. "No sound?"

"Unfortunately not. The chat room is frequently used by unscrupulous people wanting to make some money. These people don't care how they earn it either." She breathed deeply through her nose. "Somebody is running scared and posted this as some kind of insurance."

"Could it have been Hilga?" I asked.

"Possibly, but look." She pointed to a shadow on the screen. "There's a third person in that room. That's the person who's running scared. That's the person who filmed the meeting. I think it's a woman."

I watched as Hilga, face set with a serious expression, spun around and stormed from the room. She said something to the third person. "That's Cheryl."

"How do you know?" Lori's brow wrinkled.

"Look at the profile of the shadow. I'm a photographer. I notice these things."

Ruthie sipped her wine. "Doesn't make sense. Why would Cheryl be dating Rossi if she's afraid of him?"

"Love." Brock set a stack of files back into a box. "What if she truly loved Doyles and is trying to get revenge on Rossi? It's the plot out of a bad movie, but people have done worse things for love."

Lori clapped her hands. "You're a genius, Lisa. This is our first solid lead. I'll bring Cheryl in for questioning in the morning. As far as Rossi will know, it's in regard to Hilga's murder. In fact, I'll question him again, too. If Cheryl is the third person in that room, she needs to be protected."

"Any way I can watch the interviews?" I knew the answer, but had to ask anyway.

"You know you can't. Don't worry. I'll fill you in. Good night, folks." Lori headed to her room, once Morgan's.

"When I bought this mansion after Lauren died, I had no idea I'd fill up all the rooms. I thought they'd sit empty and look pretty," Ruthie said. "Isn't it wonderful to have a full house?"

"Yes." I smiled. "I'm following Lori's example and going to bed." I gave Brock a warm, lingering kiss and motioned for Shutterbug to come with me. Morning would come and boxes awaited. So far we'd only uncovered information we'd discovered on our own. But in my heart, I knew the key to Dad's killer was in one of the boxes, waiting to be found.

Lori was already gone by the time I crawled out of bed the next morning. In her place was Jason who'd volunteered to help on his day off.

"Hey, little sis." He grinned and handed me a cup of coffee. "You're the first one up."

"It's been a couple of late nights."

"Lori told me." He leaned against the kitchen counter. "I'm worried about her. The chief has been asking a lot of questions about where she is every day. I keep telling him she's pounding the pavement looking for Hilga's killer, but he wonders why I'm not with her more. We'll have to remedy that. She needs to keep in contact with me instead of running off on her own."

"I agree. It's too dangerous for her to spend too much time investigating alone." I'd grown fond of Dad's girlfriend and often wondered what it would have been like if she'd become my stepmother.

"Don't tell her this because she'd probably shoot me, but I followed the example she did with you and Ruthie and put a tracker on her phone and in that ugly watch she wears."

"You didn't." I snorted coffee out my nose. "Oh, she'll kill you."

"I'll remove it after we catch Rossi." He clinked his mug against mine. "Here's to insanely brilliant but clueless partners."

"Here, here." Oh, I hoped I was around when and if Lori discovered Jason's ploy to keep her safe. He might need my protection.

We refilled our mugs and moved to the dining room. I might grumble about the overwhelmingness of all the files, but by going through them, I felt as if Dad were with me in some way. So many pages filled with his handwriting were in each box. "I promise to make your killer pay," I whispered. If the roles were reversed, he wouldn't stop until he'd avenged me.

I glanced up in surprise when Lori marched into the house. "I thought you were questioning Cheryl."

"Seems Rossi took her on a little vacation to the mountains." She dropped her gun and badge on the table. "Hey, partner. I've got an hour to help you two, then I'm to write down everything I've done today. Chief Warren wants me to keep a log detailing what I'm doing at what time and how long it takes."

"What does he think you're doing?" Jason scowled.

"Not my job, obviously." She ripped the lid off a box. "I've told him I'm working on Hilga's murder. Even if he knew we were going through these boxes, he shouldn't care. Since we suspect Rossi had a hand in her death, and Kevin was investigating Rossi, it all ties together."

"Unless your chief doesn't want you to tie Rossi to anything," Ruthie said passing through the dining room on the way to the kitchen.

Lori and I stared at each other. "Did she just suggest Chief Warren might be dirty?"

"I think she did. Have you considered it?"

"Of course I have, but there's no evidence. The man lives like a pauper."

"Maybe he's saving it for retirement," Jason suggested.

I sent Lisa a text. "Let's see what Lisa can dig up on Chief Warren."

"I'm seriously going to mention that girl to the FBI when this is over." Lori set a stack of files in front of her.

"Don't you dare take away my makeup artist." Ruthie took a seat at the table. "She's too good."

"She's too good at hacking to be a makeup artist." Lori shook her head. "Imagine how much good her skills can do in the world."

As much as I would regret losing Lisa as an artist, she'd still be my friend. I agreed with Lori. Her skills were best used for the good of all and not just erasing ten years off my grandmother before she stepped in front of a camera.

I opened a file and froze. "I think we just answered our own question." I held up an old newspaper article showing a photo of a much younger Chief Warren shaking hands with a younger Rossi. "The article says Police Officer Warren was receiving a reward for bringing down a man trying to rob a casino teller." The two men definitely weren't strangers, and it made sense that this act of paying a reward might have bought a young officer's loyalty.

"How can I ask him about this?" Lori shook her head.

"Just say you ran across it while investigating Rossi," Jason said. "If he's innocent, you'll find out soon enough. If not, well, you'll know that, too. Don't do it unless I'm with you. He won't kill both of us." He grinned.

"Not funny, Jason." I punched him in the arm. "We're being serious."

"I'm serious about her not questioning him alone." He shrugged. "He's already suspecting you of doing something in secret. If he is dirty, you'll have a great big target on your back. That's not as likely with both of us. These men seem to only like the odds when the other person is outnumbered."

"Okay. We'll ask him about this tomorrow." She snapped a picture of the article with her cell phone. "From now on, we work under his scrutiny, only reading the files and anything not exactly in the line of our job during off hours. Sorry, Kelly. These files are all on you. Good find."

"I'll keep at it. I'm learning a lot more about who my father really was. A good man and a good cop."

Tears shimmered in Lori's eyes. "The best." She collected her things and left, promising to be back by dinner time.

I shed a few tears of my own before digging back into the box in front of me.

Chapter Seven

"They lawyered up." Lori threw herself into the dining chair next to me hard enough to topple over. "As for the chief, absolutely nothing. I asked him about the photo, and he glared at me until I grew uncomfortable enough to leave his office."

"Now what?" I sipped my third cup of coffee of the day. With all that's going on, my mind had raced most of the night leaving me drained this morning.

"You ask that a lot." She scowled.

"Because, my dear friend, you told me I have a tendency to run off half-cocked. I'm trying not to do that." I grinned around my mug.

"You're also a smart mouth." She smiled, then sighed. "Maybe you'll have better luck with Cheryl." She jabbed a finger in my direction. "But, I did not say that. What I will say is I know she goes to the spa every Friday. Today is Friday. I also know she sits in the sauna for at least fifteen minutes."

"Ah, I guess I'm going to the spa."

"You'd better get a move on. She'll be in the sauna in thirty minutes."

"Thanks for the last-minute warning. Ruthie, we're going to the spa. Now."

My grandmother blinked vacantly at me from the kitchen, then nodded. "All right. I'll get my purse. Lori, let Morgan know where we went."

A minor miracle, but we were out the door ten minutes later. Ruthie saw no point in getting dolled up just to have mud slapped on her face. I agreed.

We parked and raced inside. Ruthie to get her own pampered treatment, me to don a white towel and hit the sauna. I hated saunas. I wasn't a fan of the eucalyptus mist or the overbearing heat, but I'd sacrifice for the cause.

Pretending not to see Cheryl, the only occupant in the sauna, I entered and took a seat opposite her. I leaned my head back and closed my eyes.

"Kelly?"

I popped them open. "Hey, Cheryl. Sorry. Didn't see you."

"I'm usually alone in here this time of day." Her tone said she preferred today be an alone-day. Too bad. I was here to see what I could dig out of her.

"Sorry. It's the only time I had free. Busy hunting for a killer. You know—same old, same old." I flashed a grin.

Holding tight to her towel, she scooted closer to

me. "You shouldn't." She got up. I thought she was leaving, but instead she peered through the window.

Was she going to kill me? What a way to go.

She resumed her seat and fixed me with a serious stare. "You aren't here by accident. What do you want?"

"If you didn't have anything to do with Hilga's death, why get a lawyer?"

Her lip curled. "I forgot you're friends with that cop. Look, I have my reasons for being with Rossi. Your involvement will only get you killed."

"Rossi had something to do with Robert's death?"

"Mildred killed Robert. You know that."

"Yes, I was there when she tried to kill me. I was also in Las Vegas when thugs showed up at my rental. Oh, and don't forget the all-important fact that Robert owed Rossi a lot of money. Either you're a cold-blooded gold digger, or you're out for revenge." I leaned closer to her and lowered my voice to what I hoped was a sinister warning. "We have a video of you filming an argument between Rossi and Hilga." I stood and approached the door, then glanced over my shoulder. "You could be in grave danger, Cheryl. Don't be an idiot. Talk to Detective Lawrence." I pushed against the door.

"Wait."

I turned and raised my eyebrows.

"You're right. About everything. Rossi doesn't know about the video. I filmed them through a tiny camera in a necklace I wore. That was when he threatened Hilga if she didn't hire me on as a client."

"Why would he care?"

She gave a wry smile. "Because he fancies himself in love with me. I can pretty much get him to do anything, unless he discovers it's all a ruse."

"Did he kill my father?" I held my breath, waiting for her answer.

"I don't know. I don't even have proof he killed Hilga. She'd signed me, so why kill her?"

Good question. "That's something I need you to find out."

"I can't just ask him. He'll kill me."

"Then wrap him around your little finger and trick him into saying something incriminating." I marched over and gripped her hands. "I need your help, Cheryl. Please. I truly believe he's responsible not only for Hilga's murder but my father's."

She stared up at me, then nodded. "I'll try. I can't promise any more than that."

"I'll take it. Thank you. See you on the set in a couple of weeks."

"I want something in return."

"Name it." I crossed my arms.

"You had no acting experience, yet were thrust into a leading role. You've won a major award. I want you to coach me."

I did not expect that. "I've never had any training."

"That's my point." She set her jaw. "Train me or I don't do any snooping. Starting today."

"Okay. Meet me at my house after lunch." I'd need time to hide all the boxes. Maybe Sarah would let us do our digging in her cottage.

After hitting the shower, I spent time on an aqua

massage table and waited for Ruthie's facial to finish. I texted Brock and asked him and Morgan to move the boxes to the garage if Sarah didn't have room. On the way home, I explained about training Cheryl.

"Good. I need something to do. I have way more experience than you do. We'll coach her together."

Hopefully, Cheryl would be fine with that. My grandmother could be a bit overbearing, and that was putting it mildly.

The boxes sat on one side of the three-car garage. Sarah had been emphatic about not filling her cottage with boxes that could attract a killer. "Been there, down that," she said. Either way, the boxes were out of sight. It would be easy enough to drag in a couple of portable air conditioners and turn the larger area into a work space.

Sarah audibly groaned at finding out her ex-husband's mistress would be spending time at our house. But, being the good person she was, she headed to the kitchen to prepare lunch for our guest.

When Cheryl arrived, Sarah propped a foot on a stool and gestured at the buffet table. "Enjoy."

"What's wrong with your chef?" Cheryl popped a strawberry into her mouth.

"She's Robert's ex-wife." I filled a plate. "Ready? We can take our food to the patio. Leave your cell phone, purse, and all jewelry in the house." I wasn't taking any chances on Rossi planting some kind of listening device on her.

"I'm not the one he broke up with her for." She followed me outside after leaving behind the required items. "I don't know where to start, so I brought several outfits to change into. Why did I have to take off my jewelry?"

"Don't be ridiculous." Ruthie laughed. "An actor can make the clothes work. If you're good enough, you can make the audience believe a pair of holey jeans are appropriate for a black-tie event. As for leaving the other things in the house, well, you need to be as blank a canvas as possible."

"Is she going to be here the whole time?" Cheryl jerked her thumb toward Ruthie.

"Of course," I said. "We're a team." Although without a doubt, my grandmother would drive not only Cheryl but myself to distraction. I couldn't help but wonder if the starry-eyed, movie-star wannabe would still love acting when the coaching was over. "Where did you tell Rossi you were?"

"I told him the truth." She bit into a piece of melon. "I'll be lying so much over the next few weeks, being truthful as much as possible seems wise. Your chef is much better than I ever was."

"Young lady, you were a horrible cook." Ruthie shook her head. "If not for Robert's stipulation in his will, Lana would have fired you after the first day."

Her face darkened. "I'm not sure I can do this with her here." Cheryl faced me. "I'll need to concentrate, and she's mean. No coaching means no spying."

I sighed. "I don't want to be mean, but if you want to take this seriously, we'll have to be brutal on you. You've signed a contract to act in our award-winning crime drama. You need to know how to act or you'll ruin our ranking." I bit into a chicken salad sandwich and glanced to where Brock and Morgan exited the garage.

They converged on the food like starving animals. Cheryl immediately turned into a giggling, eyelash-batting dummy. Good luck, sweetheart. Brock was mine.

After lunch, Ruthie ordered the men into the house saying Cheryl didn't need an audience. They shrugged and went in to find a sports program on TV.

"Okay, girl. Stand there on the pool deck," she said. "You're playing a rookie cop, so act tough." She handed Cheryl an old script of ours. "You'll read Kelly's part."

Cheryl looked like an animal confronted by a predator. She gripped the script with both hands. "Um, from the beginning?"

"That's always the best place."

"Be nice." I turned the script to a section of dialogue between Ruthie's character and mine. "Here, we're discussing the fact I was almost killed and woke up in an alley. You'll need determination, a bit of fear, but most of all guts. Put yourself in the shoes of the character and inflect those emotions into your reading. Don't be afraid to act it out."

She started reading. No inflection, no emotion, nothing. It sounded as if she were a scared schoolkid giving a book report.

Applause behind us caused her to stop. "Rossi." She forced a smile.

"Well done, darling. You're a star." He faced me. "Thank you for this gift to my girl."

"What are you doing here?" Cheryl closed the

script.

"You didn't answer your phone." His eyes hardened.

"That would be my fault." Ruthie unfolded herself from the lounge chair. "We wanted absolutely no distractions or props. Her personal effects are on the coffee table." My grandmother was so smooth it was no wonder she'd been nominated, and won, several acting awards.

"Yes, well." He exhaled heavily. "I've come to take you to a meeting with Louie Stock. He wants to talk more about your character."

"Now?" Her eyes widened.

He nodded, then glanced at Ruthie and me. "If you'll excuse us, Cheryl needs to gather her things."

"Not a problem." I rose to my feet and started clearing the dishes. "We can resume tomorrow at the same time."

Rossi held back as Ruthie and Cheryl entered the house. "What kind of a stunt are you playing at, Miss Canyon?"

I stiffened, then straightened and faced him. "I don't know what you mean. I saw Cheryl at the spa and she asked me to coach her since she's going to be in the same series I'm in. There's nothing underhanded going on here. Of course, you'd know all about underhandedness, wouldn't you?"

He gripped my arm. "You're playing with fire, little girl."

Yanking free, I narrowed my eyes. "Don't touch me again. There's nothing going on here. You must have a guilty conscience. Is that it?" I brushed past. "Have a nice day, Mr. Rossi."

My skin prickled as I felt his gaze on my back when I entered the house. I turned and flinched at his angry expression. Still, a tinge of pride filled me for standing up to the lion and walking away unscathed. I wanted him to know I was on to him. Eventually, I'd push him against a wall, and he'd do something stupid.

Chapter Eight

A few weeks went by with Cheryl appearing sporadically for her acting lessons, always with Rossi in tow. The man didn't seem to trust me any more than I trusted him. We'd reached a stalemate. Now, we'd returned to filming, and time for snooping would be limited.

On the upside, I could glean information on the relationship between Louie and Rossi. The crime lord had to hold something over Louie's head for our director to allow someone as poor at acting as Cheryl onto the set, in what could turn out to be a major role in our television drama. To make the taste in my mouth even fouler, Rossi also popped in and out of the studio like a demented jack-in-the-box. His presence made everyone edgy.

During a scene where I only appeared for a

moment, I sat back and pretended to watch Ruthie interact with the new rookie, Cheryl. But I was actually watching the subtle mannerisms of Louie and Rossi—one intimidated, resembling a mouse stalked by a cat. Way more interesting than any show on television.

By lunchtime, I figured the best course of action was to corner Louie in private. While Rossi and Cheryl headed for the cafeteria, I followed the director into his office.

"Go away, Canyon, I'm busy." Louie plopped into his leather chair.

"Doesn't look like you are." I grinned and sat across from him. "Why did you agree to let Cheryl in our show? She doesn't have a smidgeon of acting ability."

"None of your business." He rubbed both hands roughly up and down his face.

"As the second top-billing actor on the set, I think it is my business." I leaned forward, piercing him with my stare. "How much did Rossi pay you?"

"He didn't pay me anything. There's no mystery here, so poke your nose somewhere else."

I crossed my arms. "You're lying. You know I'm like a pit bull when I latch onto something."

"More like a rat." He sighed. "You don't know what you're snooping into."

"I think I do. Shall I tell you?"

He shook his head and scribbled something on a sheet of paper. He slid the paper across the desk and put a finger to his lips. "Not here," it said. He motioned his head for me to follow, and we headed out of the building.

Weaving in and out of trailers, Shutterbug close on our heels, we entered a trailer that had been closed for renovations. As soon as Louie closed the door, he whirled to face me. "Are you completely insane? Do you know who Rossi is?"

"Maybe, and yes. Is your office bugged?" I leaned against an outdated, 1970s harvest gold counter.

"Why do you bring that dog everywhere?" He glared at Shutterbug.

"Because she's a great warning system, and she's my service dog."

"You don't need a service dog."

"The tag on her collar says otherwise." I smiled. In order to take our pets with us wherever we went, Ruthie, Brock, and I had gotten our dogs certified. With my talent for trouble, I needed a guard dog. "Stop changing the subject. What does Rossi have on you?"

"Gambling debt." His shoulders slumped. "I'm an idiot."

I refrained from agreeing or disagreeing. "How much?"

"So much I'm in danger of not paying alimony."

I winced. His ex-wife, Marie, was not the type to miss an alimony check. "So, he's absolved your debt because of Cheryl?"

"Yeah, but he likes to hold it over my head. The man loves to play games." He gripped my arm. "He's a killer, Canyon. Stay away."

I would if he had left my father alone. Rather than say anything, I kept my gaze locked on the tortured face of my director.

"I'm outta here." He shoved me away and stormed from the trailer.

It didn't take me long to realize I was now alone, other than my dog, on the outskirts of the studio. If attacked, no one would hear me scream. I darted out the door like the rat Louie compared me to and sprinted for the cafeteria. I was nosy, but not stupid. The more I snooped, the more I needed to be around a lot of people for my own safety.

Heads turned as I barged into the room, banging the door against the wall. I gave a sheepish grin and got in line to purchase something to eat. When I joined my family at a table, Ruthie narrowed her eyes.

"You're all sweaty."

"Went for a run." I mouthed "later" to Brock's questioning glance. "I'm finished filming for the day, so no big deal. After I eat, I'll head to the trailer to remove my makeup." And fill Lisa in on the new development about Louie.

I gave Brock a quick kiss, then took my lunch to my makeup trailer. The place was empty, so I took a seat at the small round table and ate my chef salad. Louie wasn't a poor man, so for him not to have enough money to pay alimony because of a debt owed to Rossi had to be a huge debt. Our director could also be in mortal danger if he didn't pay. Robert Doyles was a prime example.

"You look deep in thought." Lisa sat across from me.

"I didn't hear you come in."

She laughed. "Obviously."

I filled her in on my conversation with Louie.

"Have you found out anything new?"

"Rossi doesn't have a rap sheet. Not even a speeding ticket." She tilted her head. "You need to be searching the backgrounds of every chief-of-police since your dad. Someone is being paid off."

I nodded, having suspected as much myself. "Lori is looking into that. We've gotten through half of my father's boxes and it's apparent we've some dirty cops involved. Haven't found a document yet that tells us who he suspects, but I'm sure there is one."

"Or you've not seen it because it's in code. Do you want me to come over and see if I can find out if you've missed anything?"

"It'll be daunting, but yes. If you have the time, I'd love your help." I threw away my cardboard container and moved to the makeup chair. I could remove my makeup myself, but Lisa promised me a facial. While she worked, I told her about the acting lessons for Cheryl in exchange for information. "She's given us nothing."

"She puts herself in danger just by agreeing to it. If Rossi found out." She lowered her voice. "He'll kill her. He claims to love her, but betrayal would erase any emotional ties."

"She loved Robert. It's revenge for her. And very dangerous."

Lisa smeared some kind of paste on my face. "I'm falling for Lance, big time, and I'd do almost anything for him, but I'm not sure I'd become a crime boss's mistress."

Me neither. Gathering evidence and turning it over to the authorities so justice could be served was good enough for me. Problem this time was—the authorities were as crooked as a climbing vine.

Shutterbug's ears perked up. Since the hair on her neck wasn't standing straight, the person approaching the trailer was friendly.

Lori opened the door and stepped inside. "Is your trailer clean?"

"Yes, Morgan checks it on a regular basis."

"Good." She sat on the sofa. "Oh, a facial. I want one. We were right about Warren. I truly think he's on Rossi's payroll."

I straightened. "Do you have proof?"

"No, just seeing them at dinner twice this week. Why else would they be together? Law enforcement and criminals should not be buddies." She grinned. "All we need to do now is link Rossi to your father's murder, prove that Warren is on the payroll, and put them both behind bars."

"Right. Easy." I needed to get out there and snap photos of them. Maybe I could buy a high-fangled listening device from that store Brock told me about. Take a picture, make a recording, voilà—proof. "Let's go on a stakeout."

"I'll do your facial, Officer, if you let me come along. I've always wanted to."

"Deal. I've already broken so many rules I'll most likely get fired anyway." Lori sat in the other makeup chair. "I'm thinking of becoming a private detective anyway. I could still seek justice, but have a lot more freedom with what I'm allowed to do. I'll hire you to do all my online stuff."

"You're serious?" I halted Lisa's hands from wiping off the paste.

She nodded. "I've been thinking of it for a while now. Morgan will be my partner, whenever Ruthie allows him out of her sight. When we catch Kevin's killer, I'm quitting the force." She exhaled long and slow. "There. It's been said, and I feel as if a weight has been lifted off my shoulder."

I couldn't help but feel jealous. I'd wanted to be an investigative journalist for as long as I could remember. Instead, I acted in TV shows and wrote books of crimes I'd helped solved. "If you ever need a photographer—"

"You'll be the one I call." She leaned back. "Maybe I'll start my own company."

I laughed. "High aspirations."

"Might as well dream big. I cannot believe how much better I feel."

I examined my feelings, happy to realize my jealousy was small. I was good at acting and writing. Maybe I'd turn to directing one day. I smiled and moved to the sofa while Lisa worked on Lori. Yes, I'd learned to be happy in my career.

"Can I tell you two a secret?" I picked up a magazine, opened it, and peered over the top while I grinned like an idiot.

They both glanced at me.

"Brock and I are getting married."

"What?" they said in unison.

"We're waiting until the excitement of Ruthie's wedding dies down."

"That's sweet," Lisa said. "Wow. You're marrying Brock Hanson. Lucky girl."

"We've been together for a year, Lisa." I lowered the magazine, my smile staying in place. "You'd have to be living in a cave not to know I'm with Brock." I still had a hard time believing it myself.

Speaking of the handsome man, he joined us in the trailer, and I melted under his kiss. While he was occupied, I motioned to the others to keep quiet. We weren't ready to announce the news yet, and I was pretty sure Brock would want to do so together.

He pulled back and gave me a slow, sexy smile. "What are you gals up to?"

"Planning a stakeout tomorrow night." My heart did somersaults.

He frowned. "All three of you?"

I nodded.

"Okay. As long as Lori is going with you, because I'm headed out of town again. We're filming in Vegas this time." His eyes twinkled. "I'll do a little snooping while I'm there."

"You'll be careful?"

"Extremely." He lowered his lips to my ear. "I have you to come home to. You told them, didn't you?"

My eyes widened. "How can you tell?"

"They both have goofy grins on their faces."

I laughed. "Yes, I couldn't help myself." I peered around him. "But they're going to keep our secret, right?"

They nodded, but I was pretty certain it would be in the *Tribune* by morning.

Chapter Nine

Ruthie found out about the stakeout and exited her room dressed all in black with a beanie on her head and a backpack over her shoulder. "Gun, taser, wine, and snacks," she said. "Oh, and water bottles for you three wooses."

"Give me your gun." Lori held out her hand. "I'm not getting into a car with a loaded Ruthie Canyon."

Morgan glanced up from a ball game on TV. "You should let me go with you."

"No room, sweetie." Ruthie gave him a quick kiss. "Your sister can protect us."

He didn't look convinced, but turned back to the game. "Take the dogs."

"All of them?" Her eyes widened. "Brutus should stay and watch over you. He's too big."

"Fine. I've trackers on all your phones. Keep them on you." He grinned without glancing up. "Oh, and I'll start on those boxes after this game."

"No privacy." Ruthie glowered.

"Let's go." The last thing I wanted was for Ruthie to start grumbling about how marriage tied her down. She loved being married, and now was no different than before, but if she thought her independence was being curtailed, she'd complain for hours. As it was, she'd grumble if nothing happened during our stakeout. Lori was certain the two men would meet again since they met every Tuesday and Thursday it seemed. Tonight was Thursday. "Thanks, Morgan. Since you were Dad's partner once upon a time, you might see something we skipped."

"Where are we headed?" I asked, climbing into the front seat of a rented sedan. Lori, worried that Chief Warren would recognize her vehicle, had rented an ordinary, dark-colored car that looked like a hundred others. Ruthie would share the back seat with Lisa, Sassy and Shutterbug.

Lori drove us to a small hole-in-the-wall Greek restaurant with enough windows to allow us to see inside. She parked between a pickup and a van, then we settled down to wait.

We didn't wait long. At eight o'clock sharp, a police cruiser stopped on the side of the restaurant, followed a few minutes later by Rossi's black Mercedes. The two men entered the restaurant separately, but headed to a table without waiting for the hostess to seat them. It was quite clear they were regulars.

"I had this delivered today." I handed Lori a recording device that looked like a handheld satellite dish.

"Awesome. Rich people have the best toys." She opened the window just enough to aim the device at the restaurant and zeroed in on their table No good. It only picked up jumbled conversations and the clattering of dishes.

"I'm going to have to get out and plant this directly outside where they're sitting." She opened the car door. "Hang tight." Keeping low, she headed for the trimmed juniper bushes outside the building.

I watched as she propped the device in the bushes, staying as low as possible, then she sprinted back to us and turned on the listening device she'd set on the dash.

"She's a nuisance," Rossi said. "No matter how many times she's been warned, she keeps asking questions. I saw her with Louie."

"He is her director."

"They're talking about me," I whispered.

"No need to whisper." Ruthie patted my shoulder. "They can't hear us."

"Right." I settled back in my seat.

"I can't have her killed," Rossi said. "It'll be too suspicious."

"I can arrest her."

Rossi shrugged and glanced out the window. I froze, thinking he could see us, but he turned his attention to the waitress. "Gyro."

"Accident?" Warren asked after placing his order for a cheeseburger.

"Maybe."

Ruthie slapped the back of the seat. "Go arrest them, Lori."

"For what? We can't prove they're talking about Kelly. They need to mention her by name."

They'd be too smart for that. One thing was certain, though. I'd be watching my back for any signs of an approaching *accident.* "I want Morgan to check our vehicles each time we go anywhere. I don't put it past them to blow us up."

"No." Lori lifted a pair of binoculars to her eyes. "That wouldn't be an accident. It'll be something more subtle. Something you wouldn't see coming."

"You aren't making me feel any better."

"He'll probably make it look like a mugging gone bad," Lisa said. "When you're out jogging. Maybe a crazy fan. Something like that."

"I think you should stay in the house." Ruthie patted me again. "That's the safest place."

"Unless they set the house on fire," Lisa pointed out. "That could look like an accident. If I was them, that's what I would do because it would take out the boxes and you. Double threat."

"I'm done." I clicked my seatbelt on. "Let's go home."

"They aren't finished." Lori shook her head. "They stopped talking long enough to eat, but they're going to make a plan to take care of you. I know." She tapped her temple. "Genius, remember?"

I sighed. At least I'd know how I would die. Hopefully, it would be quick.

A tap on the back window had us shrieking like little girls. Jason grinned in at us and stepped around to Lori's side. He motioned for her to roll down the window.

"Had a call that some women were spying from the parking lot of this establishment. Would you know anything about that?" He laughed.

"You can be such a jerk." Lori shoved open her door, knocking it against him. "I could have shot you."

"I don't see a gun in your hand. What are you ladies up to?" He reached in and petted Shutterbug.

"Surveillance."

He glanced through the restaurant window. "Be careful. If Warren sees you…in fact, he'd better not see me or he'll ask questions." He swallowed hard, sending his Adam's apple bobbing. "He'll see the report."

"You can't lie," Lori said. "Come on, ladies. We're eating Greek tonight. Ruthie, take off that silly beanie. If he wants to know what we're doing, tell them we're planning Kelly's wedding."

"Wedding?" Ruthie planted her hands on her hips and glared. "When were you going to tell me?"

I shot Lori an exasperated glance. "We were waiting until the shine of your wedding had died off."

"Sorry," Lori said. "It was the only reason I could come up with to explain why we might be sitting in a car before heading inside. Got it, Jason?"

"Yep. Wedding plans. Congratulations."

"Thanks." I couldn't stay mad. I was getting married.

Since the weather was gorgeous, we left the windows open and kept the dogs in the car.

Shutterbug would bark like mad if we needed to be warned. With my heart in my throat, the four of us women entered the restaurant.

As the hostess led us to a booth near Rossi and Warren, the men glanced up, wearing identical scowls. Less than five minutes later, they paid their bill and left with to-go boxes in hand. The cold stare Rossi cast my way left me shaking.

Lori watched them drive away, then went to retrieve the listening device. "I'm keeping this as evidence, even though they didn't mention you by name. We might still be able to use it."

"If we can pin anything on Rossi," Ruthie said, "and if we can get a jury to hear that. The judge might dismiss it from the record, but the jury will still have heard it. You can't erase what you've heard." She nodded, her brows raised. "See? You learn a lot from watching television."

"We're done here." Lori dropped a five-dollar bill on the table even though we didn't order anything and marched back to the car.

By the time we returned home, Morgan had the boxes piled against the garage walls and papers spread across two six-foot tables placed side by side. "I cracked the code, kind of." He grinned up at us. "Oh, and I'd love to give you away at your wedding, Kelly. Your father would be proud."

I shook my head at Ruthie. "Seriously? Did you text him from the car?"

"Yes."

"You all do realize that Brock wanted to be part of the announcement, right?" I turned back to Morgan. "What did you find?"

"Look. I thought to myself, how would Lisa look at these files?" He flashed her a smile. "I realized upon closer inspection that your father's handwritten notes didn't make any sense. No full sentences, misspelled words—"

I should have caught that. "Dad was a great speller."

"Right. So, I started playing around and realized that every third letter makes a word. I found Sawyer's name, Chief Warren's name, a rookie we once worked with…he's dead now, and here is Rossi. Kevin always called him Soprano. You know, on account of the show."

"I step back as second genius." Lisa clapped her hands. "You're brilliant."

"You would have figured it out given time. You hadn't pored through these yet." Still, red dusted his cheeks and his chest swelled a little bigger. "I'm going to make copies of these pages once I've finished cracking the code and send it to a buddy in the FBI. It'll take a while, so you'll need to stay out of harm's way, Kelly."

"Too late," Ruthie said. "We heard Rossi and Warren planning for an accident to take care of her."

He looked stricken. "You don't go—"

"Anywhere alone, I know." My cell phone rang. Caller ID showed Brock. I tossed the others a wave and headed for the pool area for some privacy. Just me, my man, and my dog. "Hey, Babe." I stretched out on a lounge chair.

"Hey, yourself, gorgeous."

"How's filming?" With my free hand, I petted

Shutterbug and played with her big ears.

"Good. How are things there?"

"Well, Lisa let it slip that we were getting engaged, then Ruthie told Morgan, so basically all of Hollywood will know by morning."

"It's already on twitter." He laughed. "I'm sure Susan Gilroy is writing an article on how our secret is out as we speak."

I laughed with him. "Do you mind so much?"

"No. I'll put a ring on your finger the minute I get back. So, what are you keeping from me?"

"What do you mean?"

"There's always something you don't want to worry me about when I'm not there."

I closed my eyes. He knew me so well. "Rossi and Warren are planning on an accident to get me out of their hair."

Silence.

"Hello? Brock?"

"Trying to digest this. Where's Morgan?"

"Oh, he found a code in Dad's files. Isn't that great?"

"I'd like to speak to him."

I sighed. "Hold on." I carried the phone to Morgan, watched as he spoke to Brock, who gave a sharp nod, then handed the phone back to me. "Well?"

"He's hiring you a full-time bodyguard," Brock said.

Chapter Ten

A six-foot-tall, blond Amazon with a gun showed up on our porch at daybreak. I didn't understand, nor want, a bodyguard other than Morgan, but here we were.

"Nadia Popov." She pushed past me and slammed the door. "You are actress, Kelly. Good show. Coffee?"

"Uh…" I glanced at the kitchen, saw no sign of Sarah, then thrust my cup toward Nadia.

She grimaced. "I prefer black."

"Sarah?"

"I'm here." She handed Nadia a mug. "My, you're a big girl."

"Big bones." She moved to the wall of windows that overlooked the backyard. "I do not like this. Anyone can see." She yanked the door open, dropped her mug, shattering it on the patio and dragged a yelping Susan Gilroy from the top of the fence.

"Wait." I rushed to the woman's aid. "She's no threat."

"Spy?" Nadia raised one finely arched brow. Really, the woman was beautiful and fierce enough to grace the cover of *Vogue*.

"No. Sorry. My new bodyguard is a bit over zealous."

Susan rubbed her arm. "I see that. Did you get a chance to see the *Tribune*?" She smiled. "I brought you a copy, just in case. You should have told me about your engagement."

I grabbed the tabloid from her hand. "It isn't official yet." There we were in full cover. She'd used a photo taken at Ruthie's and Morgan's wedding. "At least we look good."

"Brock always looks good." Susan grinned. "Anything else for me?"

"No. Pretty quiet around here." I set the tabloid on a patio table.

"Then why do you need a bodyguard?" She peered up at Nadia.

"Brock insisted."

"You're looking into Hilga's murder." She drew out the word murder. "And you've had threats against you."

"Do not print that in the paper. I'll sue you for libel. Lots of actors have bodyguards." I plopped on the lounge and tried to ignore the hovering Nadia who watched without expression as Sarah cleaned up the shattered mug.

"Fine. Let me know when you have crumbs to give me." With one last look at Nadia, she left through the back gate.

"You'll be on the front page in the next edition," I told the giant.

Nadia made a noise in her throat, then smiled, making her even more striking.

Morgan and Ruthie joined us.

"My friend." Nadia wrapped Morgan in a hug. Ruthie wasted no time breaking them up.

"Nadia, this is my wife, Ruthie. Darling, this is the daughter of a friend of mine. We served in the army together. When her father died, Nadia took his place as bodyguard for hire."

Ruthie must have decided the woman was no threat at stealing her husband. "It's nice to meet you. Thank you for watching over my granddaughter."

"I am huge fan of your show." Nadia nodded. "It is my pleasure."

Now that the niceties were out of the way, I said, "We've got to get to the set."

"I will drive." Nadia strode into the house and out the front door, leading Ruthie and me to a black jeep with tinted windows. Morgan would stay behind to keep working on Dad's code.

We introduced her to Lisa, then let Nadia search the trailer although we told her Morgan kept it free of electronic bugs. None of us wanted to be the one to cross her or argue the point.

"I'd like to get my hands on her face," Lisa said. "Prettiest skin I've ever seen. She's like a giant porcelain Barbie doll."

Louie must have thought the same thing because he was struck dumb at the first sight of her. I rather liked him speechless and hid a grin as I took my place on set.

Nadia stood off to the side, her back against the wall, her gaze darting from door to door. She stiffened at the sight of Rossi, but made no other expression. Curious. She obviously knew him or of him. She barely spared Cheryl a glance.

After we'd shot our first scene, Louie approached Nadia. "Ever do any acting?"

She shook her head and looked down her long nose. "No."

"I could hook you up with an agent."

"No."

Face beet red, he turned and shuffled back to his director's chair. Poor thing. He'd really wanted to impress the Russian.

Nadia followed Ruthie and me to the cafeteria and ordered enough food for herself to feed three people. With a smile, she led the way to a table in the corner, took a seat facing the door, and dug in. I cast an amused glance at a shocked Ruthie.

"How do you stay so shapely if you eat like that?" She asked.

Nadia shrugged. "I work out three hours a day. You will have to also since I must watch you."

Ruthie and I groaned in unison. "No, thanks," I said. "We'll just watch. I prefer a morning jog."

"We will do that too." She waved a hand and continued eating. "Then, you will tell me why bad man like Rossi is allowed anywhere near you."

"You know him?"

"I do. He kills and steals like a predator. He killed my father."

My hand paused my fork halfway to my mouth. "Mine too."

"Then we take him down together."

Fresh hope sprang up in my chest. There was no way Rossi was walking away this time.

Speaking of the devil in a dark Armani suit, Rossi, along with Cheryl, headed for the lunch line. He cut a quick glance at us, but no look of recognition for Nadia flickered across his face. Very telling that he could have someone killed and not know of the family the deceased left behind. I'd been brought up not to hate, and that vengeance belonged to God, but this man challenged the good things I'd been taught. While I didn't want his death on my hands, I thirsted for justice and would do everything in my power to see that happen.

After eating, we headed back to the trailer to have our makeup refreshed and to change into the clothes we'd wear in the next scene. Days of shooting two scenes were rare, but with Louie preoccupied with trying to impress Nadia, he'd loosened up on the tyrant attitude.

Lisa glanced up from her laptop. "Your father was undercover in a Las Vegas sting and killed."

"You are spy?" Nadia narrowed her eyes.

What was with this woman and people being spies? "She told us at lunch. Lisa is a genius with research and hacking. She's a spy of the internet, not espionage." I took my seat in the chair while Ruthie changed into black slacks and a long-sleeved shirt. We'd be filming a fall scene outside.

"Make sure I don't sweat off the makeup," I said. "I'm going to swelter."

"Seriously?" Lisa gave my hair a tug. "I know how to do my job."

"Sorry."

After making a sweep of the trailer again, Nadia sat on the sofa. "You can find anything?"

"Pretty much, given time," Lisa said. "What do you need?"

"Evidence."

"Okay. I'll look for your father while digging on Kelly's."

"I find you bodyguard. What you do is dangerous."

"How long have you been in America?" I tried to turn my head, but Lisa still had a firm grip on my hair.

"Five years. I live in Russia. My mother and father split when I was little. I knew him through letters and phone calls, the occasional summer trip." Tears welled in her eyes, only to be angrily swiped away by the back of her hand. "When I found out he died in car accident, I hired an investigator. His brakes had been cut. I vowed revenge and worked on getting my visa to come here. I took over his company and voilà."

Ruthie and I changed places. Shutterbug followed me to the backroom and watched as I changed into slacks, a blouse, and a blazer. I got hot just looking at the clothes. I'd just slipped the blazer on when the side of the trailer was riddled with…something not as loud as bullets, but loud enough to cause me to shriek and dive to the floor.

"Stay," Nadia yelled. The next thing I heard was pounding footsteps.

I wasn't going to lie there like a broken doll when someone had lured away my bodyguard. I pushed to my knees and peered out the window. Paint splatters covered the glass. Why would someone shoot at us with paintballs? I pushed to my feet and joined Ruthie and Lisa in the front room.

Nadia returned with a young man. She slapped the back of his head and shoved him onto the sofa. "Talk."

"I don't know anything." The man paled. "I pick up garbage. Someone slipped me a box. Inside was the paint gun, one hundred dollars, and instructions to shoot this trailer. I figured it was a joke between actors."

Nadia raised her hand again to strike him, then lowered it. She leaned close enough for their noses to touch. "Who?"

"I swear I don't know. The box was in my locker. Ask the custodian, Rod."

We needed to check on my friend right away. Rod would never accept a bribe to harm me.

Chapter Eleven

After sending a messenger to let Louie know we'd be late for filming the next scene, we borrowed a golf cart and went in search of Rod. All the while I prayed he'd be okay. Almost a year ago, his best friend had been murdered for getting involved with the wrong people. I didn't think Rod would make the same mistake, but Rossi proved to be a fierce convincer.

Nadia drove like a Nascar racer to the point I made her stop long enough for me to let Shutterbug loose. The dog would have to run after us where she'd be safer.

"You aren't worried about us?" Ruthie asked, clutching a side rail for dear life.

"No." I flashed a grin over my shoulder and held on tight. "Ready."

Nadia blasted us across the lot. "This is fun."

"Speak for yourself," Lisa said.

Rossi stepped from Cheryl's trailer.

Nadia aimed for him, swerving at the last minute. Her laughter almost drowned out his cussing. "Sorry," she muttered. "Not really," she said to the rest of us.

I shared her sentiment, but not at the expense of a crash. "Stop in front of the cafeteria. I'll run in and see whether anyone has seen Rod." When the cart stopped, I raced inside to find Mary.

The cleaning lady looked up from wiping down tables. "Hello, stranger."

"Hey, Mary." I felt a twinge of guilt at not making more of a point to seek her out once in a while. She'd been a big help in the past when I needed a spy. "Have you seen Rod?"

"He was eating in the staff lounge a few minutes ago. Let me check for you." She set down her rag and exited through a side door, returning a few minutes later. "They said he's on the lot somewhere. If I see him, do you want me to give him a message?"

"Tell him I'm looking for him. It's important." I hurried back to the others. "He's supposedly out here somewhere."

"Louie is going to be out of his mind," Ruthie said.

"I'll have Nadia blow him a kiss." I grinned at the Russian. "He's smitten with her."

Nadia glowered. "I have no time for romance until vengeance is complete." We sped forward. "Then, I do not want a man a head shorter than myself."

I shrugged. We shared one aspiration. Her romantic notions were hers. I had one thing on my mind at that moment and it was Rod.

We zoomed past Louie who posted his hands on his hips and shouted something I couldn't hear. Ruthie thought maybe he said filming was canceled. I chose to go with that idea. Sometimes playing dumb or misunderstanding seemed the best option.

After searching for half an hour and finding no sign of Rod, worry changed to fear. It wasn't like him not to be available. We should have seen him fixing or cleaning up something. My throat swelled.

"There he is." Lisa pointed to our right where Rod exited a storage shed.

I jumped from the cart and rushed toward him. "Where have you been? I've been worried sick."

He pursed his lips and looked past me. "Who's the giant?"

"My bodyguard. Answer my question." I crossed my arms.

"Working, as always." He locked the door to the shed. "What's got you all worked up?"

"Someone shot our trailer with paint balls."

"Okay, put in a work order, same as anyone else." He tilted his head. "You've been shot at with real bullets. This is literally child's play to you."

"The young man said someone put a box in his locker. He suggested you might know something."

"That new kid? The gopher?"

"I don't know who he is, Rod. Did you put a box in his locker or not?"

"Sure I did. Since I was headed that way, the

regular delivery guy asked me to drop it off."

"What's his name?"

"Dan. I can take you to him. What's going on? Why do you need a bodyguard? What in the world are you into now?"

I lowered my voice. "Finding out who killed my father."

He scratched his chin. "Suspects?"

"Rossi." I resumed my seat.

He paled. "Girl, you scare me. Let's go." He hopped onto the back of the golf cart and hung on. "I'll pretend I knew about you ladies taking one of the carts. Head to the west end of the lot." He yelped as Nadia bolted forward.

Dan was a huge bear of a man, well over six feet tall with skin the color of ink. White teeth flashed in his face as we drove up. "I've not seen anything this pretty in a long time. It isn't often I see a cart full of beautiful women."

The way Nadia giggled I figured she'd found a man that interested her. "You flatter."

"That I do, my Amazon queen." He spotted Rod. "What's up, man?"

"Do you know where that box you asked me to deliver came from?"

He nodded. "The pile of stuff to deliver, same as everything else." He reached for a clipboard and flipped through some pages. "No return address. Must have come from someone at the studio."

Dead end. We'd run all over creation for nothing. Well, unless you counted the blushing Nadia as something. We said our thanks and goodbyes, leaving Rod behind and headed back to our makeup trailer.

"Rossi could have easily dropped the box with the other mail," I said, falling onto the sofa. "The man seems to have free rein around here."

"Why?" Nadia straddled a chair backward. "Warning?"

I shrugged. "I guess, although he's already given me a few. What's one more? We need to talk to Cheryl without him."

"The man is on her like a tick," Ruthie said. "How do you plan on getting her away from him long enough to carry on a conversation?"

"He can't follow her to the women's restroom." A plan began to ferment. "If I can find a way to have her meet me there at a certain time—" I couldn't text, and even an inner message like the box the young man had received would be risky. I'd have to do an old fashioned slip-of-a-note in her hand as I passed by trick. "Let's go to the set."

"Okay," Ruthie said, "but I'm pretty sure filming was canceled for this afternoon."

It turned out Louie had shouted that we had filming and to hurry up and get back to the set. Oops. I wasn't sure he bought my confused dummy act either, but I kept with it. During filming, my character handed a sheet of paper to Cheryl's character. I slyly added a note for her to meet me in the restroom during a break.

An hour later, because Cheryl either couldn't remember her lines or said them with no emotion, I headed to the women's restroom and waited. Five minutes later, Cheryl ducked in. I locked the door to give us privacy.

I explained the paintball episode. "Do you know anything? Is it another warning from Rossi?"

She sighed and leaned against the counter. "I sent the warning." Her gaze locked with mine. "You have to step back. Rossi is growing agitated. When he gets like this he's dangerous and reacts violently. You're in his crosshairs, Kelly. Now that you've hired a bodyguard, Rossi knows you're on to him."

"I can't stop. Not until he's behind bars."

"Or you're in an unmarked grave somewhere. You know what he's capable of." Her voice trembled.

I knew firsthand. "Who in the police force is on his payroll?"

"Chief Warren and a couple of others. I'm not sure of their names. Your detective friend is in danger, too. I heard Rossi mention your name and hers. I've got to go." She put a hand on the door. "I'll let you know if I learn anything more." She flipped the lock and darted out.

She hadn't told me anything I didn't know other than the fact a couple of cops were on Rossi's payroll. I might not have known for sure, but I'd suspected. I gave her a few minutes to get back on set before I left the room. Luckily Rossi's back was turned as he spoke to Louie so he wouldn't be sure of what time I'd actually returned.

Nadia noticed though and didn't look pleased. I guess I should have told her I was leaving. Still, she had to realize I wasn't in much trouble if Rossi was where she could see him. But then again, he didn't do his own dirty work.

When filming finished, Rossi ushered Cheryl

from the studio. He didn't cast me or Nadia a glance. I hoped he didn't suspect Cheryl of being a traitor. That wasn't something he would forgive. Although I needed her inside information, it was more important that Lori take her into protective custody—something I mentioned the moment she arrived at the house at dinnertime.

"He'd get to her in jail," Lori said, shaking her head. "We'd have to kidnap her and sneak her into a safe house. It's near impossible with him glued to her side the way he is."

"I can lure him away," I said.

"No." Nadia pressed her lips together.

"You'd be giving your life for hers. That won't solve anything." Lori grabbed a slice of pizza from the coffee table. "We have to work together, possibly make sacrifices to make sure Rossi and his buddies get put away for a very long time."

"I'm with Lori on this one," Morgan said. "We can watch Cheryl to the best of our abilities, but you're our top priority. Brock would kill me if anything happened to you." He winked. "I'd be a little upset, too."

I smiled. It was good to be loved. "As long as Cheryl shows up to film each day, I won't worry too much."

"What do you want to do next?" Nadia leaned back and closed her eyes.

"Tonight or any time?"

"Anytime."

"More surveillance, I guess. I can't have too many snapshots of a killer. One of them might be the incriminating evidence a jury needs. In fact—" I jumped to my feet. "We should stakeout his house. Find out who comes and goes."

"Sounds good to me," Lori said. "Where's Ruthie?"

"Shower," Morgan answered. "Do me a favor and you three go before she gets out. My heart stays in my throat the whole time she's out there playing detective. My bride tends to be impulsive."

"That's stating it mildly." I hurried to my room to grab my camera bag, which held my taser, pepper spray, gun, and photography equipment. All I needed, and promised Brock I wouldn't leave home without. I rejoined the others. "Who's driving? We can't take the Aqua Machine, and Nadia's driving scares me."

"That leaves me." Lori led us out of the house to her ten-year-old maroon Corolla. "It doesn't matter if my car is recognized. The chief knows I'm doing what he's ordered me not to. I expect to be fired any day now."

"Then you can help us full-time." I gave her a playful bump with my shoulder. "No more Hollywood-street crime for you."

She laughed. "I'd make more money working for myself. But I've got to hang on at the department as long as possible. I have access to things there I wouldn't elsewhere."

True. It was a definite plus having a detective on your side.

Chapter Twelve

We parked one house down from the monstrosity Rossi purchased. Close enough to see who came and went, but far enough away to avoid drawing attention. Except for the fact that Lori's old car stuck out like a weed in a bed of daisies among the more expensive vehicles lining the street.

"We need to be able to see in the house," Nadia said.

"We'll worry about that if someone arrives," Lori told her. "The biggest part of a stakeout is patience." She opened a bag of powdered donuts and passed it around.

"These will give you a big butt." Nadia handed the bag to me.

I shrugged and took out five of the little things. "I don't have a weight problem."

"Yet." She wiggled her eyebrows.

Biting one in half, I shrugged. It wouldn't hurt me to put on a few pounds. I'd run an extra mile in the morning if I needed to.

"Get down." Lori scrunched in her seat. "Headlights."

I bent over and continued to eat. A squad car pulled into Rossi's driveway, stopped at the gate, then proceeded when the gate opened. The chief had the code to the gate. Made him guiltier in my book. I agreed with Nadia. We needed to get closer.

"If Nadia gives me a boost, I can get over that fence and snap some pictures." I pushed open my door.

"Are you nuts?" Lori faced me. "If you get caught, you're dead."

"Isn't that what we came for? Trespassing and other illegal activities?" I grinned. "Who's with me?"

"I am." Nadia wasted no time joining me on the sidewalk.

"Yep, I'm definitely going to get fired." Lori joined us and locked the car, leaving Shutterbug behind. My dog was awesome, but there was no way she could climb a six-foot wall. "Be careful, be quiet, and follow my lead. Got it?"

Nadia and I nodded. If Lori could go along with something that could end her law-enforcement career, I'd let her take the lead without argument. At least, I'd try to. Taking a back seat didn't come easy.

Before we reached the gate, we squeezed along the fence behind some manicured bushes until we reached a spot we could climb up. A decorative boulder provided a good place for the tall Nadia to stand while giving us shorter women a boost.

"What if there are dogs?" I asked.

"Keep your pepper spray handy," Lori said.

"I have steak." Nadia grinned and patted the backpack she wore. "Works every time."

Lori frowned. "You scale fences often?"

"Hmm." She tilted her head and gave a one-shoulder shrug. "Perhaps." She bent over and cupped her hands. "You first, Kelly. Then hide and wait for me."

I planted my right foot in her hands and flew through the air, landing hard in a flower bed.

"Oops," I heard from the other side.

When I'd caught my breath, I ducked behind a bush and waited for Lori to catapult over. "That woman doesn't know her own strength," she said, picking herself up and brushing off the knees of her pants. "We could have broken a leg."

"But you didn't." Nadia landed gracefully on her feet next to us. She whistled softly. When two rottweilers appeared around the corner of the house, she tossed the steaks from her backpack. "They will sleep like babies."

"As long as you don't poison them." Lori removed her gun from the holster on her belt. "Follow me."

We jogged past the two dogs happily wolfing down the steak. They barely gave us a glance.

Only one light shone from the house. We headed that way, looking in on a living room done in blacks and reds. Filing her nails on the sofa reclined

Cheryl. In two facing leather chairs sat Rossi and Warren, both with drinks in hand.

I lifted my camera and snapped some pictures while Lori set up the recording device.

"Refill, darling." Rossi held up his glass. "Don't keep us waiting. Have the chef fix us something to eat while you're at it."

"She's off tonight, sweetheart, but I'm sure she left something for you." The smile Cheryl pasted on her face faded as she headed for the kitchen. Her lips curled, but she held her tongue.

I moved to the kitchen window and peered inside. Not seeing anyone other than Cheryl, I tapped on the window.

She whirled, a hand on her chest. Seeing me, she closed her eyes and shook her head. When she'd composed herself, she held up a finger, then opened the refrigerator and removed a tray of meat, cheese, and crackers. She returned to the living room, set the tray on the glass-topped coffee table, refilled their drinks from a crystal carafe on a sideboard, then pleaded a headache.

Rossi grabbed her hand and pulled her down for a rough kiss. "Take something so you'll feel better. I'll want your company later."

"I'll be ready." She smiled and slid out of sight. A few minutes later, she joined us in the shadows. "Are you nuts? They're in there right now plotting ways to get rid of you. Here you are right where they want you. They could shoot and say they thought you were an intruder."

"Shh." Nadia glowered. "We can't hear."

"Is there anything else you can tell us before you

head to your room?" I wasn't crazy about hearing how they wanted to finish me off, but I'd come too far to turn back now. The more evidence we had, the better chance of conviction.

"No. I'll keep you informed." She disappeared the way she'd come, and a light flickered on in a room at the end of the house, illuminating part of our hiding place.

"She's going to have to go out like her old man," Warren said. "No one is going to believe an accident. We'll have to have someone shoot her. Make it look like a mugging."

My blood ran cold. A mugging could happen anywhere, even on the lot.

Nadia put a hand on my shoulder. "I am here to keep you safe. I will go with you everywhere. Even bathroom."

"There might be collateral damage," Warren went on, "but it can't be helped. I'll see what I can come up with. Maybe one of our men can pull her over for speeding and say she went for her gun. Happens all the time. We've options."

I'd heard enough. "Let's go."

Lori nodded and put away the equipment. "I'm afraid you're going to be a virtual prisoner until this is over, Kelly."

"No, I refuse." I hurried for the fence, passed the two sleeping dogs, and waited for the others.

This time, I had Nadia boost me up and let me climb over rather than being thrown. I didn't need any more pain in my muscles tomorrow than I'd already have. Back in the car, I sat in the backseat, leaving the front for Nadia, and wrapped my arms around Shutterbug's neck. A dog brought comfort few others could.

When we arrived home, Morgan and Ruthie listened with wide eyes as I told them how I was supposed to be "finished off." Saying the words out loud didn't make them any less frightening.

"Your father wouldn't have you go this far at avenging him," my grandmother said. "He wouldn't want you to die over this."

"It's too late now. Even if I stopped snooping, Rossi wouldn't stop coming for me. I know too much." I kicked off my shoes and propped my socked feet on the coffee table. What bothered me the most was if Warren got his chance, one of the people in the room with me would also die. Most likely Nadia or Ruthie since I was rarely without them. Nadia was being paid to be at my side, but my grandmother didn't need to be in danger. "No one goes anywhere with me from now on except for Nadia. I won't risk it."

"I agree," Morgan said. "Nadia is good at what she does. She'll keep you from harm."

"Or I will die trying." Nadia grinned and sat next to me. "We are friends now, yes? Brought together by common ground."

"Yes." I linked my arm with hers, feeling a little better. Tomorrow would be a better day. Brock would be home. In fact, he should have called me by now. I checked my phone. Nothing.

I tried calling his phone, but it went straight to voice mail. Two seconds later, it rang. "Brock?"

"Yeah, I need someone to come and get me. I'm stuck on Pacific Coast Highway. My brakes failed and I'm, uh, well, let's just say my truck won't be going anywhere after kissing the median."

I bolted upright. "Are you okay?"

"Just a bump on the head, thanks to my airbags."

"We'll be right there." He gave me the mile marker and after telling the others the situation, Morgan, Nadia and I sprinted for Nadia's jeep, leaving a disgruntled Ruthie behind with the dogs, Lori for protection and an order from Morgan to stay in the house with the doors locked.

"Give Brock a kiss for me," she said.

"I will do so gladly," Nadia said. "I have crush on actor."

"He's mine, giant woman. Lips off." I shook my head and climbed into the front passenger seat.

Nadia shrugged. "We shall see."

Morgan laughed. "Ladies, let's rescue our hero and then fight over him."

"Thank you, Nadia." For a moment, she'd helped me let go of some of my fear.

"You are welcome." She patted my shoulder as Morgan sped us toward my man.

We found the truck easily enough, but there was no sight of Brock. With my heart in my throat, I called out his name, almost fainting as he stepped from behind an opened beach umbrella in the parking lot of Huntington Beach. Tears ran down my face and I leaped into his arms.

"You're bleeding." I didn't care who saw me. I kissed him and squeezed with all the strength I had.

"I'll be fine, despite someone trying to kill me in a crash. I thought the umbrella a good enough hiding spot in a pinch." He released me and folded up the umbrella, stowing it back in his truck.

"Hello. I am Nadia, and I will kiss you."

His eyes widened as she planted a rough kiss on his lips. "Hello to you too." He shot me a questioning look.

"She's my bodyguard and has a fan crush on you." I grinned, suddenly not minding that she'd kissed him. The look on his face said he was all mine. "We have quite a lot to fill you in on."

Sirens wailed in the distance.

"Nadia, take Kelly in the jeep. I'll find a ride back with Brock. You can't be here when the cops show up. We don't know which ones can be trusted. Go."

Nadia gripped me by the arm and dragged me to the jeep. Seconds later, as I kept my gaze on Brock for as long as I could, we sped back toward home.

"Don't kiss my man again," I said when I could no longer see him. "We're getting married."

"I will be in your wedding." She laughed. "I will have relationship with big man at the studio."

"You do that." Poor Dan wouldn't know what hit him.

At home, I told Lori and Ruthie what had happened. Lori immediately got on her phone and let us know that Jason was one of the officers at the scene. I sagged with relief into a chair.

"They'll be fine then." My brother would keep a close eye on Brock and Morgan. Rossi's plan had been foiled for now. I couldn't help but wonder how many more times we'd get lucky.

"When we find the list of dirty cops," I asked, "Who do we take the list to? Who can we trust?"

Lori's brow creased. "I'm looking at the district attorney. So far, I think the man is clean. If we get the information to him, enough to convict Warren, we can take Rossi down too."

"So take down Warren and get Rossi." Made sense. Now to do so without being killed.

Chapter Thirteen

Morgan called to say he took Brock to the hospital to have his head checked and that Jason accompanied them to prevent further trouble. Five minutes later, Nadia and I were back in her jeep and on our way to join them. No way was I letting my man out of my sight for another minute.

Once there, we rushed to where Brock sat stoic while a nurse stitched his head. "I'm fine." He grinned. "I know movies are fiction, but I've learned a thing or two about defensive driving."

"Thank God." I waited until the nurse had finished, then cupped his face in my hands and kissed him. "We're even on scaring each other."

He laughed. "Woman, I don't even come close to how you make me feel every time you leave the house."

"He has a concussion," the nurse said. "He'll be fine." She gathered her things and left, promising the doctor would be around soon with the release papers.

"I'm onto something," Jason said. "I can't explain it to you right now, but I'm headed back to the precinct. Your—" his gaze racked over Nadia, who seemed very interested in my good-looking brother, "friend can drive you home."

Perhaps Nadia would forget Dan and focus on Jason. I'd like to see him find someone to love. "Ready?" I glanced at Brock.

"Very. I hate hospitals." He slid off the bed, whispering in my ear as we walked out the door, "We need to matchmake Nadia and Jason."

"I was thinking the same thing." I slipped my arm through his and squeezed. "It'll be something nice to do in the middle of all this bad stuff. A feeling of normalcy."

His laugh rang down the hospital halls. "Sweetheart, this is the norm with you."

At the house, after everyone finished making sure Brock was okay and Morgan filled us in on any news—which was basically zilch—Brock said, "Okay. I know it isn't a secret, so I'm not going to waste anymore time." He gingerly lowered himself to one knee and fished a ring box from his pocket. "Kelly has already said yes, but let's make it official in front of family." He opened the box to reveal a 4-carat diamond ring in the shape of a heart. "Kelly Canyon, will you marry me?"

I smiled through my tears. "Get up, you silly goose. Of course I will." I kissed him to the sound of applause. Seconds later, the doorbell rang.

Morgan motioned us all back and peered through the peephole. "It's that reporter."

"Let her in. She won't go away until she gets what she wants." I smiled at the ring on my finger.

Susan stepped through the doorway and snapped a photo of Brock still on one knee. "Tomorrow's front page."

I helped Brock to his feet. "Were you spying on us?"

"Of course." Susan fiddled with her camera. "How else am I supposed to find out what you're up to?"

"I will tie her to a chair." Nadia narrowed her eyes and crossed her arms.

Susan's eyes widened. "For what?"

"Interrogation."

"Settle down, big girl." I shook my head. "You're a pain in my rear end, Susan. I told you I'd tell you everything when things were finished. All you're doing is putting yourself in danger."

"And I told you I won't print anything about what you're doing until you say so. We didn't mention anything about you getting engaged. This is big news." She flashed a grin and headed for the door. "Ciao, love birds." She sashayed out the door.

I sighed and plopped into a chair. You'd think she'd learned not to ask too many questions after our run-for-our-lives-through-the-woods adventure. "We need to keep our eyes on Susan along with everything else."

"We are not bringing one more person into this house." Ruthie glared. "We have no more bedrooms. Besides, every conversation we have will be front-page news in the tabloid."

Good point. Hopefully, she was waiting on news from me and not doing any investigating on her own.

I woke the next morning to a team of men in my backyard. I rubbed my eyes and squinted. Oh, heck no. I dashed outside. "Why are they putting curly barbed wire on my fence?" I glared at Morgan.

"Nadia and I decided that with the ease Susan climbs over our fence, it's needed." He didn't glance my way.

"It's ugly and looks like a prison."

"You are in prison until Rossi is behind bars."

"Does Ruthie know about this?"

"Not yet."

I stormed into the house and knocked on Ruthie's door. "You need to get up and come out here right now." I kept rapping until she came out.

"What?" She wrapped her robe tight around her middle. "We were up late last night. Can't a girl sleep in?"

"No. Not when your husband is desecrating our yard."

"What?" She headed for the French doors and froze. "Uh…"

"Yeah." I raised my eyebrows and pointed. "You need to get him under control."

"You do know who I married, right?" She pushed open the door and stepped outside.

"Sorry, babe, but this can all come down at a later time."

She took a deep breath and exhaled slowly. She

opened her mouth to speak, then closed it and turned back to the house muttering something about coffee.

I followed. "What's going through your head?"

She stopped before heading for the kitchen. "Remember how afraid I was about losing my independence when Morgan proposed? Well, I've lost it and I am not happy."

Sarah thrust a mug of coffee into our hands. "You both need this."

"Bless you." Ruthie lowered to a chair in the breakfast nook. "Don't look so frightened. I'm not dissolving my marriage or anything. I just have some adjusting to do, is all."

"Good. This isn't permanent." I glanced out the window at our prison wall. "At least the men can't keep us from filming. Speaking of…we'd best get a move on." I took my coffee with me to my room and dressed in yoga pants and a tee shirt. Lisa would have her work cut out erasing the effects of a long night from my face.

With all the humans and dogs, we had to take two cars. Nadia drove me and Brock in her jeep and Morgan drove a silent Ruthie. Lori had gone to work to dig through more information and would meet up with us later. With all that kept happening, Morgan hadn't made any more progress on breaking Dad's code.

I saw another long night in our future. Those files needed to become our top priority.

"I found some information on a couple of the officers working under Warren," Lisa said the instant we walked into the trailer. "I've already sent the info to Lori. I'm betting the men are on Rossi's payroll." She handed me a list of three names. "They've all been transferred due to behavioral issues, such as police brutality, tardiness, and insubordination."

"Definitely sound like the type of men Rossi would hire." The fact they now worked under Chief Warren made them all the more suspect. Solving Dad's murder became more difficult each day.

When Lisa finished with my makeup for the day, I headed for the studio, leaving Ruthie to follow later. I filmed without her for the first scene and saw no reason to make Louie upset by causing him to wait.

The director was nowhere to be seen. When I asked, the cameraman motioned toward Louie's office. I raised my hand to knock and stopped at the sound of loud voices on the other side of the door.

"She's one of my best actors," Louie said. "There's no way I'm doing anything to jeopardize that. Nor will I allow you to."

"I'll do whatever it takes to get her off my back," Rossi replied. "And so will you if you know what's good for you."

"Threaten me all you want. I'm through with this whole thing."

"You owe me a lot of money, Stock."

"I'll sell the house. You'll have your money in thirty days. Now, get off my back."

"You really think your ex-wife will relinquish the house?"

"It's in my name. She won't have a choice."

Footsteps had me scurrying to take my place on

the set. I waited behind the ugly metal desk used for my role and pretended to thumb through a magazine.

Louie's door opened and Rossi stormed out. I kept my eyes down, peering up from under my lashes as he glanced my way. The moment he left the building, I sprinted for Louie's office and closed the door, leaving Nadia to stand guard.

"Oh, good grief. Woman, you're the thorn in my side." His face darkened. "Do you have a death wish?"

"It might appear so. Thank you, Louie, but I can't have you sell your house. How much do you owe Rossi?"

He crossed his arms and leaned back in his chair. "Three-hundred thousand dollars. I have the money, just don't want to hand it all over to him at once. I've sold some stocks and stuff. By saying I'd sell the house, I can get Maria somewhere safe and buy myself some time. I don't expect to live through this. Not with a man like Rossi."

"Don't say that." I reached across the desk, only to have him withdraw further. "I've got some things in the works. I will see him pay for the things he's done."

"Good luck." He let his chair fall back to all four legs. "We've got work to do. Look properly chagrined, as if I've scolded you. We'll need some explanation as to why you're in here, in case Rossi came back."

"Does Cheryl film today?"

"Yep. She's late."

When Cheryl didn't show up by the time Ruthie

arrived for her scene, worry flooded through me. She hadn't arrived on the set nor had Rossi returned. By lunchtime, I'd worked myself into a tizzy over what could have happened.

"She'll be fine," Brock said while we ate in the cafeteria. "Rossi can't harm her. It'll be too suspicious."

"Like your brake line being cut?" The more we backed the man into a corner, the more he'd act violently. Eventually, he wouldn't care who he took out as long as he took out as many people as possible before an iron-barred door slammed behind him.

Somehow, I needed to draw Rossi into the open. Too many people were in danger. I'd need to set a trap with myself as bait. I glanced at Brock. He'd never allow it. Still, I'd find a way to put an end to the danger surrounding my family.

"Don't even think about it." Brock tossed his napkin onto his half-finished salad. "We're all in this together."

Darn the man for reading my mind. He'd been able to see right through me from day one. "I want this to be over."

"We're getting close. You have a list of potentially dirty cops. Morgan is working on breaking your father's code. Nadia has joined our team." He started to take my hand, but smiled. "See? There's Cheryl. She's fine."

My gaze darted to where Cheryl and Rossi entered the cafeteria. No amount of stage makeup could cover the bruise on her cheek. I narrowed my eyes and met the cold stare of Rossi.

Chapter Fourteen

Louie cursed at the sight of Cheryl's face. "What happened?"

"I slipped on the pool deck and hit the corner of a table." She took her place on set.

"We'll have to make sure to film only the good side of your face." He shot Rossi a dirty look.

Jason barged into the studio and marched up to Louie. A moment later, he motioned to Ruthie and me. "We have to go."

"Filming is canceled for today," Louie said. "Cheryl, go take care of your face."

We followed Jason to the parking lot where Brock and Morgan waited. Nadia stood behind us like a sentry.

"Lori is missing," Jason said. "I haven't heard from her since last night, and she didn't turn up for work."

"Did you try her apartment?"

"Of course I did." He scowled. "That's the first place I looked. Then I went to your house. Nothing there but a fence I didn't expect to see."

"Maybe she has a hot tip she's following up on." I glanced from one worried face to another.

"Maybe. Either way, you've all been put under house arrest. We can't take any chances. Nadia, take them home and make sure they stay there." A smile teased at his lips. "I'll be by later."

A pink hue kissed her cheeks and she nodded. "I will do that." She took my arm and escorted me to the jeep.

"You've stars in your eyes," I said, climbing into the backseat, leaving the front to Brock.

"He is not as tall as I would like, but he has kind eyes."

"You could do a lot worse than my brother." I clicked my seatbelt into place as we sped from the lot. I might be teasing my new friend, but worry for the woman who might have once had a chance of being my stepmom ate at me. What if she'd been run off the road? Maybe she hadn't been as lucky as Brock. I called Jason. "Did you try tracking her?"

"Of course, I did. Come on, Kelly. I know how to do my job. Her phone is off."

"Sorry." I hung up.

We drove at breakneck speed back to the house where Nadia once again took me by the arm and practically dragged me inside. I shook her off. "No need to manhandle me. I am capable of walking."

She rolled her eyes and scanned the area behind

us. "Get in the house fast. That van was not here this morning." She gave me a shove.

A white panelled van, no logo on the side, sat outside Iris Beacon's house. I smiled. She'd know whether or not the vehicle belonged there. I placed the call as soon as I got inside. "Do you know why there is a van in front of your house?"

"Hello, Kelly. No, I do not. I've been watching with binoculars, not thinking it wise to peer over the fence. They arrived soon after you left this morning. No one has come in or out since."

That didn't sound good. "You be careful. I don't think they're friendly."

"They are not." She sounded irate. "I tried taking the two young men cookies, but they refused them. Who doesn't like chocolate chip cookies? Crooks, that's who."

"You wouldn't by any chance have seen Detective Lawrence today?"

"Uh—"

"Be careful." I hung up. "Lori is at Iris Beacon's house."

"How do you know?" Brock asked, sitting cross-legged on the floor for some cuddle time with Brutus.

"I've never known her to be speechless before." I grinned. "There are two non-cookie-loving men in the van. They've been there all day."

"Which means they suspect Lori is close by," Morgan said.

I turned, not having heard him come in. "That's what I think. They most likely believe she's in here." Moving the blinds a fraction, I peered out the window. "What do we do now?"

"Let me think." Morgan paced the room. "We're in big danger if they think she's here, and she's in danger if they find out she isn't."

"I go with letting them know she isn't," Ruthie said. "Also, what if they have a listening device like Kelly does?"

We all froze and stared at her. I reached over and grabbed the remote to turn on the radio. If they did have a device, I'd just put Iris in harm's way. "I need to warn them."

"I'll find a way around back without being seen." Morgan sighed. "I check the house regularly for bugs. Didn't figure on them listening from the road."

Shots rang out across the street. The van fired at Iris's house, and someone inside the house fired back. Sirens wailed minutes later, and the van sped off.

Morgan yanked the front door open. With the rest of us on his heels, he dashed across the street. "Ms. Beacon?"

Iris, her wrinkled, still-lovely face peppered with glass, opened the door. "We're fine. Your sister is a good shot, but she got winged."

Lori leaned against the wall, a hand clasped to her side. Blood stained her fingers. "Just a graze, I think." She fell to the floor.

Morgan scooped her into his arms and hurried to his car before the cops arrived.

"Act like it was a random drive-by," I said. "I'll explain the truth to Jason when I get him alone. Iris, you need to go somewhere safe for a few days."

"I will not run from my home. I've been here too long." She lifted her chin.

"Please. Just for a few days." I put a hand on her shoulder. "I can't be worrying about you right now."

She exhaled heavily. "Fine. I have a sister in Burbank. Call me when it's free to return. I'll have someone come fix these windows while I'm gone. Be careful, Kelly. I won't be here to watch your back."

I grinned as she headed down a hallway, to pack I hoped. When Nadia reached for my arm, I held up my hands. "I can walk, remember?"

She set her lips in a thin line and nodded. "We cannot stay here."

"I'll tell the police I heard the shots and came to check on Iris," Brock said. "I'll be back with you as soon as I can."

I nodded, gave him a quick kiss, and darted back home as Morgan peeled away from the driveway. Things escalated to a point that I had no idea what to do next. It wasn't safe at home or the studio. Maybe we needed to pack up Dad's files and vanish somewhere for a while.

We locked the house up tight, turned off the radio before it gave us all a headache, and settled down to wait for the return of our men. By suppertime, I'd paced the living room and hall more times than I could count, drunk way too many cups of coffee, and finally settled in the garage, staring at Dad's files.

Picking up the page Morgan had been writing on, I recognized bits and pieces of the code. An hour later, after poring through the pages he'd set aside, I stared at confirmation that the names Lisa had given me were indeed dirty cops. Now to wait for Lori to turn them in to the district attorney.

I snapped a picture with my cell phone, sent it to my email and saved it to the infamous cloud before sending it to both Lori's and Morgan's cell phones. Now, we waited for Lori to get patched up. I searched the garage for a place to hide the paper and settled on a box full of craft supplies no one used anymore.

The sound of tires on the driveway made me hurry to the house just as Morgan, Lori, Brock, and Jason returned. "Why were you gone so long?" I asked Brock.

"A couple of the officers were giving me a hard time."

"Were their names Jones, White, or Reynolds, by any chance?"

"Jones and White." His brow furrowed. "Why?"

"Because they're on Rossi's payroll." I explained the code. "Not only them, by I found copious notes of my father's suspicions regarding Chief Warren. The question now is, why keep you distracted?"

"To find out what I knew." He fell onto the sofa. "They took me downtown, questioned me, and finally released me when my story didn't change."

"Are you okay?" I asked Lori.

"Some stitches, but we all know I can't stay in the hospital. I'm a sitting duck in there." She lowered herself slowly to the sofa. "We need a place to hide out. Somewhere big enough for all of us and those files. If we were able to crack the code, then someone else can too. They'll be destroyed."

"I have a place in the Cascades." Nadia grinned. "A cabin. It will be tight, but we can do it."

"What about our show?" Ruthie's eyes widened. "We can't abandon Louie or Cheryl, and I doubt either one of them will come with us."

"We do need to get Cheryl away from Rossi." I told Lori about the woman's black eye.

"He's escalating." Lori propped a pillow behind her back. "He's going to speed up his attacks on us. I don't want to go as far as the Cascades, but we do need to leave this house."

Brock sat silent as we debated, then said, "Why not rent a place under an assumed name? We'd have to be careful not to be followed, and leave under the cover of darkness when we transport the boxes—"

"We can rent under my name," Nadia said. "No one knows me other than the silent bodyguard."

"Excellent idea." I fetched my laptop from the office and went in search of house a little out of the way. "How's Compton? Do you think Rossi would look for us there?"

"Not a chance, and we also won't be going." Lori narrowed her eyes. "You really do have a death wish. Find a place in LA."

I shrugged. It would have helped to know that information before I started searching. "Here we go." I turned the screen so the others could see. Gated with a nine-foot fence, six bedrooms, six baths, and it's for sale or rent. Not LA, but the outskirts of Beverly Hills."

"It'll do." She nodded and leaned her head back,

closing her eyes. "Set things in motion and wake me when it's time to leave."

Ruthie glared at me. "Once Rossi is behind bars, all crime solving ends for us. I'm too old for this." She huffed to her room.

I grinned and couldn't agree more. I'd sworn from the moment I learned Dad's death hadn't been a random occurrence that I would see this through. The other mysteries had all been linked in some small way, and all roads led to Rossi.

Chapter Fifteen

After taking so many turns to avoid detection that I felt lost, we pulled through the gate of our temporary, fully-furnished home at three in the morning. Nadia and Morgan ordered everyone to stay in the vehicles until they scoped out the house, using Shutterbug as the official search dog.

Once the house was declared secure, we trooped to the bedrooms and collapsed. Due to blackout blinds, I had no idea what time it was when I awoke. Morgan had taken all cell phones and removed the batteries so we couldn't be traced. The only time he'd give them back, he said, was when we went to the studio. Turns out the sun hung high in the sky when I stumbled to the kitchen.

"Good morning." I gave Brock a warm kiss. "What time is it?"

He glanced at his watch. "Almost noon." He patted my bedhead. "Nice hair."

"No teasing until I've had my coffee." Since we'd sent Susan to live with a cousin of hers for a while, we were left to our own devices. Not a problem. I knew how to make coffee.

Lori, looking as if she'd had little sleep, joined us at the kitchen table. "I contacted the DA. We're to meet him in Redondo to transfer the files."

"Why Redondo?" I poured three mugs of coffee and started a new pot.

"Out of the way." She winced and squirmed on the hard chair. "We're meeting him at three."

"In broad daylight?" My eyebrows raised.

She shrugged. "I thought it would be unexpected."

"We'd better get going then." Brock stood.

"I think it's best if I go alone," she said.

"Nope." I shook my head. "It's all of us or none."

"We'll attract attention."

"Good. Rossi will think we're staying in Redondo."

"I have to agree with Kelly on this one," Morgan said, entering the kitchen. He grabbed a mug of his own and filled it. "We need the crime boss as confused as we can make him."

"Fine. I'm too sore to argue."

We split up to get dressed, then loaded everyone into a van Nadia had someone deliver. In big bold paint on the side of its bright yellow exterior was a bouquet of flowers and the name of a florist.

"It pays to have friends in high places," she

said, climbing into the driver's seat.

"But it's so bright." I frowned.

"Hiding in plain sight, my friend."

I shrugged and climbed into the back to sit cross-legged on the floor. "Try to drive carefully or we'll be flying around back here."

"Got it." She floored the gas pedal, sending us all sliding toward the front of the van.

Ruthie yelped.

The dogs whined.

Morgan yelled and banged on the back of her seat. "Easy. Thank goodness we gave the front passenger seat to Lori."

"Got it."

I didn't think Nadia got it as she veered around a corner and I rolled into Brock. Not a bad thing. His arms wrapped around me and we rolled together.

"Wanna make out?" His eyes twinkled.

I smiled. "Might be interesting." We rolled again, landing on my grandmother's legs.

She shoved us off. "Stop fooling around. That woman is going to kill us." She gripped a leather netting hanging from the van's side panel. "Find something to hold onto."

"If you don't slow down, we'll get stopped," Lori told our crazy driver. "We can't afford to get pulled over by a dirty cop."

Nadia slowed marginally. The woman should be a Nascar driver. She weaved in and out of traffic with effortless expertise.

Keeping his arms around me, Brock wedged us behind the driver's seat. "Minimum movement, and

I get to keep you in my lap."

I hummed with pleasure and rested my head on his chest. Other than the sofa, cuddled up next to him, I couldn't think of a better place to be.

When we parked in the garage near Redondo Beach pier, none of us could get out of the van fast enough. Nadia and Morgan stood in front of us and scoped out the area before declaring it clear.

"Act like tourists," Lori said. "I'll let you know when I spot James Winston. He'll be in disguise." She pulled a simple flip phone from her pocket and headed toward the water.

Brock donned sunglasses and pulled a cap low over his eyes. I did the same, using a floppy hat for my disguise. We didn't fool anyone, but at least we tried, should Rossi or one of his goons spot us.

I caught sight of someone I didn't expect to see. "What is Susan doing here?"

"Lori called her," Morgan said. "It's part of the ruse. If she prints an article showing us all here—"

I nodded. Made sense, kind of. Might as well use the tabloid to help us in our charade. When Susan lifted her camera, I made the pretense of trying to hide my face by turning around.

Lori increased her pace toward a man fishing off the end of the pier. She leaned against the railing, said something, then walked away. He followed her into a souvenir shop. The rest of us did the same.

"District Attorney Winston, this is Kelly Canyon. Her father is the one who compiled the files."

He held out his hand. "It's a pleasure, Miss Canyon. I'm a fan of yours. So, where are these files?"

"I'll text you the address," Lori said. "You cannot let anyone follow you. We've skirted death too many times already."

"I understand. I'll come in a U-Haul at dusk. None of the neighbors should suspect a thing. I'll also recommend you for a promotion, Detective. This is a big deal."

"Thanks, but I'll be going into private investigating." She smiled.

Once the DA had left, returning to his fishing spot on the pier, we headed back to the van. All four tires had been slashed.

"My cousin is going to kill me," Nadia said. "He loves this van."

"More importantly, where is the culprit?" My eyes darted up and down the garage. I was growing tired of Rossi's games and warnings. "Why doesn't he just confront us already? This is getting old."

"Call AAA and let's get out of here." Morgan pulled his weapon. "I've got a bad feeling."

"Maybe we should go back to the shop where it's crowded," Ruthie suggested.

I agreed with my grandmother. Our location made us sitting ducks. With Nadia and Morgan flanking us, trying not to look conspicuous with guns in their hands, we headed back to the shop where we were told after five minutes no loitering.

"Do you know who we are?" Ruthie planted her hands on her hips.

The typical surfer-looking, California beach-bum young man behind the counter shrugged. "Nope, and I don't care. Rules are rules."

"I'll take the women to the ladies room. Morgan, you take Brock." Nadia started to take my arm and stopped at the stern look I gave her.

"Okay." Morgan glanced outside, then rushed us ahead of him.

Nadia banged open the door to the restroom. "Everyone out. Police business." She tossed me a wink.

"I will not." Susan glanced up from where she applied lipstick in the mirror.

"She's fine." I put a restraining hand on Nadia.

Susan grinned, revealing a spot of crimson lipstick on her teeth. "I knew this wasn't just a day on the beach. What gives? And I'd bet my favorite pair of shoes you aren't a cop." She narrowed her eyes at Nadia. "You're a bodyguard, and a zealous one at that."

Nadia made a point of checking her weapon for ammunition.

Susan paled. "Intimidating, too."

"I can't tell you what's going on," I told her. "But suffice it to say, I'm in hot water again."

"I'll sit this one out, thank you. I've had enough adventure at your side."

"Smart move." I smiled and crossed my arms, facing Nadia. "Now what?"

"We wait for Morgan's signal."

"Which is?"

"A special knock on the door." She reached behind her and locked us in. "We both have burner phones. He'll let us know when the van is fixed and safe to use."

Susan's confidence seemed to leave her. "I'd

like out now."

Nadia shook her head. "That door remains locked until I get the signal. Make yourself comfortable."

"Where?" Ruthie glanced around, clutching Sassy. "I'm not sitting on the floor. There's no telling what's on it. This place only has two stalls, and Shutterbug takes up a lot of room."

"Did you want me to leave her outside? Because she stays with me." I put a hand on my dog's head. "Next time, we'll try to find a more upscale bathroom to hide in." I patted her shoulder.

She sighed. "When we started all this months ago, it felt exciting. Now, it's growing old."

"We found Dad's killer. It's a matter of time before there's no more investigating." I might even miss catching killers.

Two hours later, three knocks, one knock, and two more sounded. Nadia unlocked the door and stepped back as Susan barged past us, shoving Morgan aside. Without a backward glance, she darted for the parking lot.

I guess she had enough. I shrugged and linked arms with Brock. "I'm ready for this day to be over. With the DA coming for the files, all we have to do now is wait for the news that Rossi has been arrested."

"Sure." Morgan led the way back to the van. "But I doubt it'll be that simple."

It wasn't. Winston showed up as he'd said. "Rossi and Cheryl Downs have disappeared. Louie Stock has gone into hiding. I'll take these files to the office, but things have ground to a bit of a halt."

Why couldn't one thing go easy? We loaded Dad's files into the back of the U-Haul. I hated to see such a big part of him drive away, and leaned into Brock.

He kissed the top of my head. "The files are safer with Winston."

"I know." There would be less of a chance of someone stealing and destroying them. I snapped my fingers for Shutterbug to come from where she nosed around the gate.

She trotted to my side, then turned as a car slowed in front of the gate. She barked, the hair on her neck rising.

Brock tackled me to the ground as shots rang out. The car sped off.

"Are you okay?" He asked, pulling me to my feet.

"Yes, you? Shutterbug?" My dog cowered under a queen palm. "Baby girl?"

Her ear bled from where a bullet had nicked it, but she seemed fine otherwise. More scared than hurt. My heart ached for my dog. "Come on. Let's go inside." I entered the house as Lori, Morgan, and Nadia dashed out.

"Drive-by," Brock told them. "Not an accident, I'm thinking, that they shot at this house."

"Pack up. We're leaving." Morgan ushered the others inside.

"Where will we go now?" Ruthie asked. "We can't keep renting houses."

"The studio trailers. No one can get on the lot without access." I held a rag tightly on Shutterbug's ear. "It'll be tight for us women, but you two men should be comfortable in Brock's trailer."

"We can't split up." Lori said.

I shrugged. "We don't have much of a choice. It's the safest place for now." I stopped the bleeding on my dog and wrapped a gauze bandage around the injured area. "No one can shoot at us from the street, the fences are too high to climb, and no one can sneak up on us. If you have a better idea, I'm open to suggestions."

No one had any, so once again we packed up and left. I was starting to feel like a nomad.

Chapter Sixteen

Nadia, with a firm hand on Shutterbug's leash, and Morgan with a tight hold on Brutus, led the way onto the lot. Nothing seemed amiss as we made our way through the darkness to our prospective trailers.

I didn't like that an entire row of buildings separated the women's trailer from the men's, but I didn't see any way around that obstacle. None of the trailers were big enough for all of us.

"I'm scared." I stepped into Brock's arms.

He held me close, his head rested on the top of mine. "Me too, but I'll be with you as soon as we're settled in my trailer, and we'll only be apart at night. With my filming over, I'll be on the set with you each day. Think of Ruthie and Morgan—they're newlyweds separated."

I made a noise in my throat. "They have years together once this is over."

"So will we."

I hoped so, but a darkness had taken root in my heart and wouldn't go away. I raised my face. "I love you."

"I love you." He gave me a long, lingering kiss until Nadia cleared her throat.

"We're in the open, lovebirds."

I stepped back. "See you in a few minutes." I turned and followed my tall friend to the trailer. Her height made an effective shield, considering my petite frame. Yes, she was being paid, very well in fact, to protect me, but I didn't want her to take a bullet for me.

Ruthie and I would share the only room with a bed. Lori would take the sofa, and Nadia said the floor in front of the door would suit her fine.

"At least let us get the custodian to bring in a cot for you," Ruthie said.

"My legs would hang over."

"Then lots of blankets."

"Just agree to it, Nadia," I said. "She won't let up until you do." I plopped into the makeup chair. "Wait a minute. If Louie has gone into hiding, there won't be any filming."

Ruthie's eyes widened. "What are we going to do all day?"

"Puzzles?" Nadia's eyebrows rose. "I can get some, I think."

There was no way I could be cooped up all day. I could go for a jog around the lot—it was large enough—but after that... I covered my face with my hands and heaved a sigh. Boredom would be my new companion until Rossi was caught. If he'd disappeared, that could take days, weeks, years!

"Stop thinking." Lori groaned as she lowered to the sofa. "Hiding can't be helped."

"If Rossi wants me, he'll find a way over that cement fence." I glared through my fingers. "Or he could have one of his loyal goons working here."

Ruthie gasped, "We could be sitting ducks once again."

"Settle down." Lori propped her elbow on the arm of the sofa and rested her head. "Go catch up on some sleep. It's still dark outside."

I agreed. Nothing to be gained by letting myself be exhausted. I sent Brock a text saying I'd see him in a few hours and went to bed.

After tossing and turning for God knows how long, I woke to sunlight streaming through the window and a woman's voice coming from the front room that hadn't been there when I'd gone to bed. I shuffled to where I hoped coffee was brewing.

Nope. Something better. Lisa handed me a big blended mocha drink. "Thought you could use this. I had them add an extra shot."

"From the cafeteria?" I grinned.

"Yep. Heard you were under house arrest." She motioned her head toward Lori.

"You're my red-haired angel." I settled in a chair someone had brought in, noticed the pile of folded blankets, and realized I really had needed sleep. "You girls were busy."

"Ruthie insisted on a comfortable prison," Lori

said. "Her words, not mine."

"Great." Brock entered the trailer. "Hey, handsome."

"Hello, gorgeous." He kissed me. "Ready for a jog?"

"You bet. I've got a lot of pent-up energy to release. Try to keep up." I motioned for Shutterbug.

"I will be coming." Nadia said, "although I hate running."

The three of us set off, Nadia staying a few yards behind us, Shutterbug on one side of me and Brock on the other. For a while, the only sound was the thudding of our feet against the pavement. Then, the sounds of the studio coming to life filled my ears. It wouldn't be long before someone realized we were living there.

Rod sped by us in his golf cart and vanished around a corner. I motioned for Brock to head that way. For a man who always ordered people to slow down, his haste made me suspicious.

We stopped at the corner of the building and peered around. Not seeing Rod or the cart, we continued our search, finally spotting the cart in front of a newly erected storage building.

Being as quiet as possible, we approached the windowless building. Nadia put a hand to her lips and turned the door knob. Rod and Louie yelped. Marie barely looked up from where she painted her nails a brilliant blue.

Seeing it was us, Louie cursed. "What in the world are you three doing here?"

"Same as you." I grinned. "Although I am surprised to see Marie here."

"I can't take the chance Rossi will use her to get to me."

"So, you're living here?" I glanced around a comfortable furnished metal room. Maybe we should have had Rod erect us a new home.

"I realized how much my idiot husband means to me." Marie blew on her nails. "When he told me of the danger to his life, I—" she shrugged.

Louie grinned like the idiot she called him. "She still loves me."

"Is the lot now a sanctuary for refugees?" Rod asked.

"It looks that way," Brock said, his arm sliding around my waist. "Let's go get breakfast. A run makes me starved."

Never one to turn down a meal, I agreed. I paused at the door. "Let's be quiet about all of us hiding here. The secret will get out soon enough."

"We'll resume filming tomorrow," Louie said. "Life must go on as normal as possible."

Good. Work would fill the time and help keep my mind off what might come. "What about Cheryl's character?"

"She's out. We'll refilm her scenes with someone new. Your bodyguard, perhaps?" He handed her a stack of papers bound in a blue notebook.

I shrugged. Stepping in for someone who broke their contract was how I got my acting start.

Nadia said she'd give acting a try, then led the way to the cafeteria, looked inside, and ushered us in. Once we had our food, she asked, "Is acting hard?"

"It can be." I tilted my head. "I'm surprised that you agreed to take Cheryl's spot." She couldn't be any worse at acting than her predecessor.

"You will give me lessons." She cut into a thick slice of ham. "In exchange for guarding you."

"How about we cut your pay in half? You have to make a living."

Just like that, I had my second acting client. Strange how different job occupations appeared out of the blue for me. From a member of the paparazzi, to wannabe photo journalist, to actor, to acting coach. Intertwine amateur sleuth bent on vengeance and I had a well-rounded portfolio.

"Why do people always ask you to be their coach?" Ruthie asked, crossing her arms and pouting when she heard the news. "I have the experience."

"We'll coach together." I patted her shoulder, squeezing through the bodies in the trailer until I found a cleared spot to sit.

A knock on the door had us all sitting upright. Morgan peered through the closed blinds. "It's Jason." He let my brother in.

Jason cut a quick glance at Nadia, then turned to Lori. "Warren wants your head."

"It was coming." She didn't seem too concerned.

"He said you haven't been in to file a report on getting shot. Funny how he knows that since he hasn't seen you."

"Because he's behind it, I'd bet my badge. Oh, wait. I did." She smiled.

"He wants you arrested unless I bring you in to

file the report.”

“Okay.” She stood. “I should be safe enough with you by my side.”

“Not if he actually puts you behind bars,” I said.

“He won’t. I’ll threaten him with evidence. I can’t have a bigger target on my back than I already do.”

“Sis.” Morgan shook his head, worry clouding his features. “You can’t. Wait and face the consequences after he’s been exposed.”

“And have every law enforcement officer hunting me down? No thanks.” She glanced around the room. “Be careful. I’ll be back as soon as I can.”

“I have to play the part of being on Warren’s side,” Jason said, facing me. “You understand this, right?”

I nodded. “Be careful. Both of you.” I hoped it wasn’t the last time I’d see either of them. Trying to lighten the mood, I said, “Remember, you can always live among the homeless like I did when they arrested me.”

“There’s a thought.” Lori grinned. “See you by dinner.” She left without a backward glance.

I choked back a sob. Fear gripped my heart, and I turned into Brock’s strong embrace.

“Enough.” Nadia slapped her hands once together hard. “We will go over my script. It will take your mind off your friend.”

Thank God for my practical-minded bodyguard. “You’re right. We’ve work to do.”

Lisa grinned. “I will finally get my hands on your face.”

Nadia’s brows knit together. “I do not like the

sound of that."

"Makeup, my giant beauty."

Nadia didn't look as if she liked the prospect, but didn't argue. Instead, she picked up the pages Louie had given her and started to read. "This does not look hard."

"We'll see, dear." Ruthie sat on the sofa. "We can't rehearse here, though. We'll have to go to the studio. This trailer is too small."

"Okay." Nadia led the way and took her place on set as if she'd been doing it for a while.

Newfound hope for the continued success of our show took root. While I felt bad for Cheryl, knowing she longed to be an actress, I couldn't help the selfish pleasure at knowing our show wouldn't suffer because of her lack of skill.

By dinnertime, Nadia had memorized and practiced three scenes. Louie would be in heaven. At the rate she remembered her lines and her passable skill at acting, we'd be back on schedule in no time.

They were right. Continuing as if we weren't in hiding for our lives was the best course of action. I hadn't worried about what was happening with Lori all afternoon.

The worry returned when she didn't show up in time for dinner.

Chapter Seventeen

I sent both Lori and Jason texts asking for an update. When neither of them replied, I paced the trailer, weaving in and out of the others.

"Sit down. You're making us all nervous." Ruthie poured herself a glass of wine. "Have a drink. It'll settle you down."

I didn't drink, except the rare occasion, but that night warranted a small glass. "Half."

I'd just finished my glass when Jason sent his reply. "I can't be around you. Conflict of interest, I was told. Lori on the run. She will contact you when she can." I wished Lori had an angel like Sarah when she hid among the homeless as I had.

"She's smart." Brock put his arm around my shoulders. "She'll be fine."

"Right." We needed to find Rossi. My guess

was he'd returned to Las Vegas. "Who wants to go to Sin City?"

Protests rang out like bells. I refused to be dissuaded. "This has to end."

"The last time we went to Vegas, ruffians broke into our rental." Ruthie shook her head. "Have you forgotten?"

"Of course not." I set my empty glass on the counter. "I don't want him creeping up on me. I want to be on the offensive. Lisa, see if you can find out where he might be hiding."

"On it." She opened her laptop, and her fingers flew across the keys.

After his initial refusal to consider the idea, Morgan sat silent. "Maybe this isn't such a bad idea. I'm not talking about going to Vegas, but we should come up with a way of drawing Rossi back to us."

Finally someone thinking like me. "What's your idea?"

"I don't have one yet. Give me time." He stood. "Let's go, Brock. I sleep better without a lot of chatter going on around me."

Brock gave me a long kiss, then followed Morgan out of the trailer.

Morgan wasn't the only one capable of devising a plan. "Let's put our heads together and come up with a way to lure Rossi to us."

"We let him think we have your father's files," Nadia said, tapping her forefinger against her temple. "It will work."

"How can we get a message to him?" Ruthie asked.

Lisa and I said in unison, "Susan Gilroy."

I sent Susan a text asking her to come to the set tomorrow. She replied with an affirmative. "I'm off to bed. Good night."

Susan arrived in the trailer as Lisa applied our makeup for the day. She sat on the sofa, tape recorder in hand. "I have a feeling this is going to be good."

"I need you to write an article that isn't the norm for the *Hollywood Tribune*." I moved a chair in front of her and sat down.

I explained about my father's files, leaving out where they were now. I told her of Rossi's hand in my father's death and that the precinct was full of cops on the take, wisely leaving out names although she asked several times. "We want you to make it sound as if we're getting ready to turn these files over to the authorities."

Her eyes had widened to the point I wasn't sure how they stayed in her head. "You want me to write this?"

"You're the only one we trust."

She put a hand over her heart. "I'm honored. This will get me on a local paper for sure."

"You can't make it sound as if you know anything more than what I've told you. This could put you in danger if Rossi thinks you know anything more than that the files exist. Don't even use his name in the article. He'll know it's him."

"Don't worry." She stood, sliding the recorder into her purse. "No names. I'll just say that files pertaining to the death of former Detective Canyon have been found with incriminating evidence. I'll dig up some details about his murder and list those. Once this article goes to press, I'm taking a long, well-deserved vacation."

"Good." I grinned. The trap would be laid by then.

When the men returned for breakfast, Morgan scowled at hearing our plan. "It's the same one I came up with."

"You aren't the only smarty-pants in the family, dear." Ruthie kissed his cheek.

Louie was impressed with Nadia's memory. "I knew you were going to be something. Try not to upstage our stars while becoming a star yourself. Someone get this woman a contract. Ruthie, who's your agent?"

"Uh."

"We don't have one," I said.

"Why not?" He frowned. "Someone find these people an agent. Call the one Hanson uses."

Thirty minutes later, a woman who looked old enough to have ridden on the Mayflower, bustled onto the set like a little bird. I couldn't believe I'd never known that Brock's agent was Lydia Williams. She didn't take any convincing to sign us three women. In fact, she couldn't have been more pleased. Once the formalities were done, we commenced filming.

"I feel legit again," Ruthie said. "Before, I felt as if I were playing at this acting thing."

Maybe, but it had been nice not to split the income.

At lunchtime, Lori sent a text from an unknown number. "I'm fine."

Gee, thanks for the elaboration. I didn't bother replying. Knowing the detective, she'd already ditched the phone.

From the relieved expression on Morgan's face, she'd sent him a text, too. One worry down, a hundred more to go.

The *Hollywood Tribune* ran a special edition that night. Susan had several copies sent by messenger and left outside the gate of the studio. When I received the text, Morgan rushed to collect the copies and handed us each one.

No front-page picture, just bold words that read, "Hollywood's Finest Being Taken Down by Crime." *Good job, Susan.*

We were silent as we read. When I'd finished, I folded the paper and set it on the coffee table. "If that doesn't bring Rossi into the open, I don't know what will."

"The woman deserves a prize," Morgan said, "but she may have put herself in danger."

"She won't be around." I didn't know where she planned on going, nor did I want to. The less anyone knew, the better.

"Now, we wait," Nadia said. "I hate waiting."

That made two of us. I slept that night, dreaming of a face-to-face showdown with the man responsible for my father's death.

Chapter Eighteen

A pounding on the door had both Ruthie and me bolting out of bed. I slipped my feet into sneakers and grabbed my camera bag. Nadia had drilled into my head to be ready to grab and go at a moment's notice.

Morgan stood outside the trailer. "Studio's on fire. Let's go. Stay together."

We hurried out, joining up with Brock at the end of the line of trailers. Flames licked the midnight sky. Sirens wailed in the distance.

"We have to make sure Louie knows." Brock sprinted away before Morgan could stop him.

Morgan growled and followed, ordering us to stay put.

"I feel like we should be doing something," I said, hitching my bag higher on my shoulder. With not even a water hose within reach, there wasn't much three women could do except wait for the men to return.

"Kelly." Someone hissed my name.

I turned to see Cheryl peeking over the top of a trashcan. "What are you doing?"

"You've got to get out of here." She stood, revealing a bruised cheekbone and a split lip. "Rossi has lost his mind with that article. He's coming for you."

"He can't get to me surrounded as I am. How did you get onto the lot?"

She shrugged. "I don't know. I've gotta run. He'll be looking for me."

I grabbed her arm. "You can't go back to him."

"I'm not. I've a place to hide out. I suggest you do the same." She slipped free and darted into the night.

I explained to the other two what Cheryl told me. "We have to find the men and leave."

Nadia agreed. "Stay on the outskirts of those watching the fire and follow me."

She led us to Louie's storage-shed home. The door hung open. She motioned us to stay back.

"No way." I darted inside.

On the floor lay an unconscious Morgan. Other than a bump on his head, there didn't seem to be any further damage.

Tied to two kitchen chairs were Louie and Marie. Louie's head hung forward on his chest. Tears streamed down Marie's pale face. Brock was nowhere to be seen.

Nadia shoved me out of the way and felt for a

pulse in Morgan's neck. "Alive." She did the same for Louie. "Also alive, but weak. He's been shot." She pointed to a bullet wound in his side.

While Ruthie called 911, I yanked the duct tape from Marie's mouth. "Where's Brock?"

"Ow." She scowled. "Rossi took him. He said he'd be contacting you."

Nadia cut her free, then Louie, and laid him on the floor. She grabbed a scarf from a nearby table and thrust it at Marie. "Press this on his wound. We have to go. Help is on the way."

This time, I didn't protest when she yanked me out of the building by my arm. With the dogs at our side, and Sassy held tight in Ruthie's arms, we raced from the lot and squeezed into Nadia's jeep.

She stopped. "Wait. Stand back in case there's a bomb." She inserted the key into the ignition.

"You can't take the chance alone." I stubbornly sat in the front passenger seat and closed my eyes. "I'm ready."

"You're an idiot." Her grin took the sting out of her words. She turned the key.

Nothing. I released the breath I was holding.

Ruthie and the dogs scrambled into the backseat. "I really should stay with Morgan."

"He won't want you to." I turned to face her. "Don't worry. He'll come for you. Brock is the one to worry about now." I cleared my throat and blinked back tears. Rossi would hold the man I loved in exchange for me, the files, or both.

Nadia tossed me her phone. "I put a tracker in Brock's watch when he was sleeping. Find him. We can't wait for Morgan."

I scanned her apps and chose, "Find 'em," which contained thumbprint photos of each of us. I pressed Brock's face, my finger lingering a moment. A red bleep appeared. I squinted. "This looks like it's coming from our house."

Ruthie grabbed the phone. "It is. Well, that was easy."

I didn't see anything easy about any of it. My phone dinged. A text message from Brock's phone. "Come alone or he dies."

"Not an option." Nadia pressed the gas pedal.

"There's no other way. I have to face Rossi alone."

Nadia peered in the rearview mirror. "Is there a way into your house the man might not know about?"

"Of course there is. The previous owner spared no expense to escape the paparazzi if she wanted to." Ruthie went on to explain about a hidden gate behind the far hedge. "Actually, the entire hedge is a tunnel."

"Why didn't I know this?"

"I never thought we'd need it. I love publicity."

Nadia stopped the car a half a block away from the house. "We go on foot from here. Kelly, you will drive to the house alone. We are taking Shutterbug so she can lead us straight to where you and Brock are."

I nodded, my heart in my throat, and moved to the driver's seat as she and Ruthie stepped onto the sidewalk. "Call Jason. Have him bring backup he can trust." I put on my sunglasses with the recording camera. "I'm going to get Rossi to admit that Warren is on his payroll. If something should happen to me, the glasses will be on the coffee table. He won't expect me to set a trap in plain sight."

Leaving them staring after me, I drove home and parked as close to the house as the driveway would allow. After slipping my taser into the back of my waistband, I slung my bag over my shoulder and approached the front door. I quietly turned the handle.

Rossi's loud voice reached me the moment I entered. "Where are the files?"

Brock didn't respond.

A peek into the living room stopped by heart. His beaten, bloodied face revealed a stony expression and a hard glint in his blue eyes. Strong to a fault, my man.

Rossi raised the gun, prepared to again strike Brock with the weapon.

"Stop hitting him. I'm here." I moved into the room, dropping my bag on the corner of the sofa and removing my sunglasses. As I set them on the table, I pressed the button. "The files are in a storage unit. We aren't stupid enough to leave them here." I longed to kill the crime lord with my bare hands.

Rossi whirled and narrowed his eyes. "I don't believe you. You don't strike me as the type to let something that important out of your hands."

I shrugged. "I don't care what you believe. Feel free to search the property."

"I already have. You've ruined me. I ought to shoot you now."

"Do it." I forced a grin, acting way braver than I felt. "You'd never see the files then."

"I could shoot Hollywood's golden boy."

"And bring down the wrath of the industry?" I widened my eyes in fake shock. "Even you wouldn't be so foolish."

"Where's that bodyguard of yours?"

"You said to come alone. I snuck out and left her to fight the fire you started."

He laughed. "Cheryl started that fire. That little lady will do anything I tell her."

Showed what little he knew. "Are you okay, Brock?"

He nodded. "You shouldn't have come, Kelly."

"I had no choice."

"How touching. Sit down." Rossi motioned toward the sofa. "Toss me your bag."

"It's my camera bag."

"You won't be taking any pictures."

I handed him the bag.

He glanced inside and removed my gun. "Stupid woman." He slid it across the floor where it stopped against the sliding glass doors.

"Can I ask you something before you kill us?"

"Ask away." He laughed. "I know this is the part of the movie where the killer spills his guts. You want to know if Warren is dirty. Yes, he is, as are several others. I'm sure you already know that from the files you've squirreled away. Am I right?"

I nodded. "But why kill my father?"

"He knew too much and became a big problem." He said it so coldly and matter-of-factly that I wasn't sure how to respond.

Shutterbug jumped against the glass, snarling and barking. Silly girl. She didn't understand how to be sneaky. At least there was no sign of Nadia or Ruthie.

Rossi whirled and fired the gun. Shutterbug yelped and darted out of sight.

I whipped the taser from my waistband and lunged forward.

He yelped as electricity bolted through him and fell to the floor twitching like a fish on the end of a line. I kicked the gun out of the way and yanked the cord off the window blinds. "No one shoots at my dog." I tied his hands behind him.

Satisfied he wasn't going anywhere, I grabbed a knife from the kitchen and freed Brock.

"I'm going to sit here for a minute, if that's alright." He fell forward onto the floor.

"Where's it hurt?" I gave Rossi a hard kick before kneeling next to Brock.

"Everywhere. Just bruises. Maybe a cracked rib. I need to catch my breath is all." He smiled through bloody lips. "You are something else."

"Hey, I don't play a tough cop without picking up some tips." I moved to stand over Rossi as Nadia and Ruthie thundered out of the kitchen.

"You took him down alone?" Nadia's brows rose.

"Piece of cake." The adrenaline left me, and I collapsed onto the sofa as Jason and Morgan ran through the open front door. "All the evidence you need to lock him and the others up is with the district attorney and on the recording in those sunglasses."

Jason gave me a long look, then nodded, before replacing the cord from the blinds with handcuffs. "Let's go. You won't see outside of prison for a very long time."

The look Rossi shot my way sent shivers down my spine. I giggled and wiggled my fingers at him. "Bye."

Brock made his way to my side and sat groaning next to me. "Can we be done with the crime solving? I'm getting too old. I'd rather not get beaten for real anymore."

"I agree with you one-hundred percent. I say we get married on the beach next weekend."

He leaned his head against mine. "That's the best idea you've ever had."

"We can't plan a wedding in a week." Ruthie's voice rose.

"Everyone I care about attending is in this room. Morgan, will you give me away?

He put a hand over his heart. "My honor."

Ruthie clapped. "Then let's get busy making plans."

"Tomorrow, grandma. Right now, I'm taking Brock to the hospital." I helped him to his feet and out the front door where Shutterbug met us. I was relieved to see she was scared, but unharmed. "We'll be right back, girl. Go watch over the others."

Despite the overwhelming exhaustion weighing me down and the worry over injuries Brock might be keeping from me, I couldn't help the smile on my face. Next week, I'd be Mrs. Brock Handsome.

Epilogue

I may have wanted a simple wedding, but word got out and Huntington Beach was packed with fans. Dressed in a simple, flowing white gown that flirted with my bare feet, and a simple flower wreath on my head, I slipped my arm through Morgan's. *Can you see me, Dad? I'm marrying the man of my dreams.* Oh, I wished he could have been there.

I glanced up at Morgan's face. He wasn't my father, but he was the closest thing I had, and I treasured him as a grandfather. Not that I would ever call him that. I got lucky every time I called Ruthie grandmother. This strong man wouldn't want to be reminded of his age.

"Next to marrying Ruthie, walking you down the aisle, or beach, is the greatest honor." Tears glistened in his eyes. "Brock is a lucky man."

"No more so than I am to be marrying him." I smiled and hugged his arm. Violins began to play and I took my first step toward my groom as the fans parted like the Red Sea. At the end, camera flashing, stood Susan Gilroy, her face split with a huge grin.

Next to her stood Ruthie, Lori, Sarah, and Lisa, the wonderful women in my life. But my gaze locked on my groom wearing all white. White dress shirt, white linen trousers, wind-mussed hair, he was the most gorgeous thing I'd ever seen. Behind him, the setting sun highlighted the ocean with waves of gold. Who needed arches and flowers when God's handiwork couldn't be topped?

Morgan slipped my hand into Brock's, then joined Ruthie. A local pastor, also dressed casually, read us our vows. I must have responded at the appropriate times, but I couldn't tear myself away from Brock's face. He still showed signs of his beating, and we'd both carry internal scars for the rest of our lives, but we would do so together.

As one, we leaned forward and kissed. Cheers erupted when the pastor introduced us to the crowd. White rose petals rained upon our heads as tears streamed down my cheeks. I was Mrs. Brock Hanson.

The End

Dear Reader,

I hope you've enjoyed this mystery series set amidst the glitter of Hollywood. I've portrayed the movie star life a bit dark, I'm afraid, and must come clean that I really have no idea how things work in Hollywood other than what I've seen in movies. I've been to the Hollywood Walk of Fame and met many of the characters portrayed there, but I've never done any acting other than skits at Vacation Bible School.

I hope you'll allow me leeway to add or subtract from reality to tell my stories. It's been a fun time! Stay tuned for the future series set in a tiny-house community.

If you enjoyed this series, you might like the Shady Acres series where a retirement community is anything but laid back and quiet. You can read the first chapter of *Beware the Orchids* below.

Go with God and keep on reading,

Cynthia Hickey

Beware the Orchids

1

Dressed in a black and white dress, adorned with a red sash and matching gardening boots, I marched through the front doors of Shady Acres retirement community to begin my new job as gardener slash event coordinator. The boots were to help me look the part. One phone call stating that I had been a third grade teacher and they'd hired me sight unseen. The director had laughed and said if I could handle thirty rowdy children I should be able to handle a retirement home of adults.

"You must be Shelby." A woman around the age of thirty met me at the door. "I'm Alice Johnson, esteemed manager and all around crazy woman. You have got to be the prettiest gardener I've ever seen."

"Thank you." I think. Her gaze flickered to my thin legs then back to the mound of black curls that wouldn't stay tied in a ponytail to save my life.

"You aren't bigger than a minute." She narrowed her eyes. "Are you sure you're up to the task?"

"Gardening has been my hobby for years, and you don't need to be big to plan events and plant flowers."

"True enough. Let me show you to your cottage and around the grounds. Then, you'll know where to park and unpack." Alice, dressed in a spotless suit of grey with a pink scarf tied around her neck, led me through a marble-floored foyer and through another set of double glass doors into a garden in desperate need of pruning and trimming.

A plump bottom and two legs stuck out from underneath a juniper bush.

"Maybelle Smith!" Alice propped her fists on her hips. "Crawl on out of there."

"Can't. I lost my teeth."

I bit my lip to keep from grinning. "Do these kinds of things happen often?"

"All the time." Alice tapped the older woman on the back. "Your teeth would not be under a bush."

A chubby woman with rosy cheeks and silver curls crawled from the bush and stood up, brushing off the knees of her knit pants. "I've checked everywhere except the outhouse."

"We don't have an outhouse, Maybelle. Perhaps you mean the greenhouse?"

"Yes. The place where flowers grow." She gave a toothless grin. "I'll go there now." She bustled off.

I couldn't help but let a giggle escape. "She's adorable."

"She's a menace. If she can't find her teeth, she'll steal someone else's. She's always where she doesn't belong." Alice continued down a flagstone path, her heels clicking in military precision. "You'll need a boatload of patience to work here, Shelby. I'd introduce you to some of our other characters, but I don't want you forming any opinions until you get to know them yourself. Here we are." She unlocked the door to a pretty little white cottage with a green tiled roof and pink climbing roses over the doorway.

I stepped inside my new two bedroom home. I could be very happy here. Wicker furniture filled the living room. A small glass table and four chairs took up the kitchen nook. In the master bedroom, a brass four-poster bed covered with a white Battenburg comforter invited one to lay back and relax. "It's beautiful."

"We did promise a furnished place, but if you want to substitute with anything of your own, just let us know and we'll have a volunteer switch it out for you, or Heath McLeroy, our handyman will help."

"Did I hear my name?"

I turned and lost all thought as a Chris Hemsworth lookalike strolled into my cottage. I closed my mouth so he didn't think I was a drowning fish. If this was the volunteer, I'd have to come up with a lot of reasons to use his services.

He grinned. "I'll be more than happy to help you with anything you need."

Oh, my, Father in heaven. Had I spoken my thoughts out loud? "Oh, well, I, uh…" I fished my keys from the little red purse hanging over my shoulder. "The red Volkswagon convertible is mine. Do you mind?"

"Not at all." He took the keys and ducked back out.

I sagged against the door. Be still my heart. I might have recently gotten out of a relationship, but my eyes deceived me into thinking I might be interested in the hunky handyman.

"Yes, he's very pretty. Most of the women here are ga-ga for him no matter how ancient they might be." Alice pointed at a stack of papers on the table. "Read over these, please. It gives your duties in great detail. If you have any questions, I'm number 2 on your phone. I'd best go help Maybelle find her teeth. See you at dinner, promptly at five."

I lowered myself into the nearest chair and flipped through the papers. Not too bad, once I got the garden in order. I had to plan a monthly grand event, a weekly social, and daily activities to get the residents out of their rooms and mingling. Alice wanted me to oversee the event she had planned for tomorrow. Bingo.

I wondered if the residents would like some of the games third graders played. Oh, well. A few moments on the internet and I'd have some ideas.

"I'm guessing you want help unloading the car?" Heath carried in a large suitcase. "And a small moving truck just pulled up. I directed them back here."

I jumped to my feet. "Yes, thank you." I had no idea where I would put all my things. It looked like most of it would go in my mother's garage after all. The clothes would have to somehow fit in the closet. Perhaps I could turn the second bedroom into a giant walk-in closet. "Just put everything in the guest room." I pulled five dollars out of my purse and held it out to him.

He laughed, the sound deep and rumbling. "I don't take tips." He shook his head and, still laughing, headed to the back bedroom.

Great, Shelby. Way to make an impression. I headed for the small kitchen, surprised to find the refrigerator fully stocked. There were no dishes in the cupboards, as I'd specified, so plenty of room for my cheery yellow and blue plates. A girl needed to be surrounded by pretty things, right? No plain white for me.

Soon, my little cottage was packed with two other muscular men and I was running out of space. Maybe I could use some of my things as prizes for Bingo. I had several stuffed animals I no longer needed, given to me by Donald. A bracelet, a necklace, the list was long of items he'd given me and I would do well to get rid of. Sweet. I had a plan.

"That little room is packed." Heath leaned against the table. "My cottage is a few doors down. If you need anything let me know. See you at dinner." He flashed another breath-stopping grin and followed the movers out the door.

The man was going to be a distraction. One I didn't want. After five years with Donald, I didn't want to think about another man. Heath would make that vow near to impossible to keep.

Having a good idea of my job duties, I decided to stroll the gardens and check out the greenhouse before heading to the dining room. At one time, someone had put a lot of work into the Shady Acres garden. The flagstone path alone was a labor of love, showcasing blues, greens, and gray stones. The evergreen bushes would be divine trimmed into exotic animals. I'd taken a class on that one summer and couldn't wait to give it a whirl. Overgrown rose bushes and other flowers simply needed pruning or replanting. I rubbed my hands together. I'd have my lovely striped boots dirty in no time. Good thing they're made of rubber. Any job goes easier if you look and feel good.

The greenhouse rose in the distance. The sun's rays sparkled off the glass like diamond dust. I pulled open the door and stepped into the musty interior.

Orchids! I rushed down the aisle, cradling a blossom between my fingers. This is the job I was born to do. While teaching had been fulfilling, I'd thought nothing of breaking my contract and paying back the remainder after Donald ditched me. I should have gotten into gardening a long time ago. Plants didn't reject a person. No, they filled the world with their beauty and scent.

I made note of where the tools I'd use were kept, where the water spigot was and turned to leave when I caught sight of Maybelle's feet sticking out from under one of the work benches. Her dirty fingers were curled around a small hand-held gardening shovel. "Lost your teeth again?"

No answer.

"It's me, the new gardener and event coordinator, Shelby. Do you need help?"

Maybelle didn't move.

My nerves tingled as I squatted next to her. Lying on its side was a box of rat poison. "Maybelle?" I grabbed her legs and pulled her out. Her lips were pulled back in a grimace over gums too swollen to hold the teeth lying loose in her mouth. I stumbled backward and screamed.

www.cynthiahickey.com

Cynthia Hickey is a multi-published and best-selling author of cozy mysteries and romantic suspense. She has taught writing at many conferences and small writing retreats. She and her husband run the publishing press, Winged Publications. They live in Arizona and Arkansas, becoming snowbirds with three dogs. They have ten grandchildren who keep them busy and tell everyone they know that "Nana is a writer."

Connect with me on FaceBook
Twitter
Sign up for my newsletter and receive a free short story
www.cynthiahickey.com

Follow me on Amazon
And Bookbub
Shop my bookstore on shopify. For better price and autographed.

Enjoy other books by Cynthia Hickey

Misty Hollow
Secrets of Misty Hollow

Deceptive Peace
Calm Surface
Lightning Never Strikes Twice
Lethal Inheritance
Bitter Isolation
Say I Don't
Christmas Stalker
Bridge to Safety

Stay in Misty Hollow for a while. Get the entire series here!

The Seven Deadly Sins series
Deadly Pride
Deadly Covet
Deadly Lust
Deadly Glutton
Deadly Envy
Deadly Sloth
Deadly Anger

The Tail Waggin' Mysteries
Cat-Eyed Witness
The Dog Who Found a Body
Troublesome Twosome
Four-Legged Suspect
Unwanted Christmas Guest
Wedding Day Cat Burglar

Brothers Steele

Sharp as Steele
Carved in Steele
Forged in Steele
Brothers Steele (All three in one)

The Brothers of Copper Pass
Wyatt's Warrant
Dirk's Defense
Stetson's Secret
Houston's Hope
Dallas's Dare
Seth's Sacrifice
Malcolm's Misunderstanding
The Brothers of Copper Pass Boxed Set

Time Travel
The Portal

Tiny House Mysteries
No Small Caper
Caper Goes Missing
Caper Finds a Clue
Caper's Dark Adventure
A Strange Game for Caper
Caper Steals Christmas
Caper Finds a Treasure
Tiny House Mysteries boxed set

Wife for Hire – Private Investigators

Saving Sarah
Lesson for Lacey
Mission for Meghan
Long Way for Lainie
Aimed at Amy
Wife for Hire (all five in one)

A Hollywood Murder
Killer Pose, book 1
Killer Snapshot, book 2
Shoot to Kill, book 3
Kodak Kill Shot, book 4
To Snap a Killer
Hollywood Murder Mysteries

Shady Acres Mysteries
Beware the Orchids, book 1
Path to Nowhere
Poison Foliage
Poinsettia Madness
Deadly Greenhouse Gases
Vine Entrapment
Shady Acres Boxed Set

CLEAN BUT GRITTY Romantic Suspense

Highland Springs

Murder Live
Say Bye to Mommy

To Breathe Again
Highland Springs Murders (all 3 in one)

Colors of Evil Series

Shades of Crimson
Coral Shadows

The Pretty Must Die Series

Ripped in Red, book 1
Pierced in Pink, book 2
Wounded in White, book 3
Worthy, The Complete Story

Lisa Paxton Mystery Series

Eenie Meenie Miny Mo
Jack Be Nimble
Hickory Dickory Dock
Boxed Set

Hearts of Courage
A Heart of Valor
The Game
Suspicious Minds
After the Storm
Local Betrayal
Hearts of Courage Boxed Set

Overcoming Evil series
Mistaken Assassin
Captured Innocence
Mountain of Fear
Exposure at Sea
A Secret to Die for
Collision Course
Romantic Suspense of 5 books in 1

INSPIRATIONAL

Nosy Neighbor Series
Anything For A Mystery, Book 1
A Killer Plot, Book 2
Skin Care Can Be Murder, Book 3
Death By Baking, Book 4
Jogging Is Bad For Your Health, Book 5
Poison Bubbles, Book 6
A Good Party Can Kill You, Book 7
Nosy Neighbor collection

Christmas with Stormi Nelson

The Summer Meadows Series
Fudge-Laced Felonies, Book 1
Candy-Coated Secrets, Book 2
Chocolate-Covered Crime, Book 3
Maui Macadamia Madness, Book 4
All four novels in one collection

The River Valley Mystery Series
Deadly Neighbors, Book 1
Advance Notice, Book 2
The Librarian's Last Chapter, Book 3
All three novels in one collection

Contemporary

Romance in Paradise
Maui Magic
Sunset Kisses
Deep Sea Love
3 in 1

Finding a Way Home
Service of Love
Hillbilly Cinderella
Unraveling Love
I'd Rather Kiss My Horse

Christmas
Dear Jillian
Romancing the Fabulous Cooper Brothers
Handcarved Christmas
The Payback Bride
Curtain Calls and Christmas Wishes
Christmas Gold

A Christmas Stamp
Snowflake Kisses
Merry's Secret Santa
A Christmas Deception

The Red Hat's Club (Contemporary novellas)

Finally
Suddenly
Surprisingly
The Red Hat's Club 3 – in 1

Short Story

One Hour (A short story thriller)
Whisper Sweet Nothings (a Valentine short romance)

www.ingramcontent.com/pod-product-compliance
Lightning Source LLC
Chambersburg PA
CBHW070307120726
47910CB00007B/2390